THE SIXTH SPELL

A PARANORMAL WOMEN'S FICTION ROMANCE
NOVEL

MICHELLE M. PILLOW

MICHELLEPILLOW.COM

ABOUT THE BOOK

You can always go home...but sometimes home won't let you leave.

At forty, Kari Grove knows she should be over her strict childhood. The grandparents who raised her had never been loving people. But some feelings are buried deep and contain more dark secrets than even she realizes.

Even after death, it would appear her grandmother isn't done controlling her life. (and that's putting it mildly)

With the help of new friends and a love interest her grandparents would have hated, Kari must finally learn to stand up for herself and unravel the tragic mystery of her past.

Heather, Vivien, Lorna, and Sue are back! With the help of Grandma Julia's ghost, they're kicking supernatural butt and taking names.

ORDER OF MAGIC SERIES

Second Chance Magic
Third Time's A Charm
The Fourth Power
The Fifth Sense
The Sixth Spell
The Seventh Key
The Eighth Potion

Visit MichellePillow.com for details!

AUTHOR UPDATES

Join the Reader Club Mailing List to stay informed about new books, sales, contests and preorders!

michellepillow.com/author-updates/

To my husband, John.
Thank you for all you do.
I love you.

AUTHOR NOTE

Being an author in my 40s, I am thrilled to be a part of this Paranormal Women's Fiction #PWF project. Older women kick ass. We know things. We've been there. We are worthy of our own literature category. We also have our own set of issues that we face—empty nests, widows, divorces, menopause, health concerns, etc—and these issues deserve to be addressed and embraced in fiction.

Growing older is a real part of life. Women friendships matter. Women matter. Our thoughts and feelings matter.

If you love this project as much as I do, be sure to spread the word to all your reader friends and let the vendors where you buy your books know you want to see a special category listing on their sites for 40+ heroines in Paranormal Women's Fiction and Romance.

Happy Reading!

Michelle M. Pillow

PRAISE FOR MICHELLE M. PILLOW

For Books in the *Order of Magic* Series

"[T]he cast of women and their bond resonates. This is a delight." *Publishers Weekly*

"The perfect combination of spine-tingling magic, paranormal fun, and the strength of female friendships. Michelle M. Pillow delivers an emotionally powerful, must-have read." - *K.F. Breene, Wall Street Journal, USA TODAY, and Washington Post Bestselling Author*

"Michelle M. Pillow's Second Chance Magic proves that sometimes all it takes to get a second chance after a massive betrayal, is a little luck, a lot of magic, and the help of your best friends." - *Mandy M. Roth, NY Times & USA TODAY Bestselling Author*

"Second Chance Magic starts with a bang and does not slow down! It's a beautifully written story of starting over and finding your inner power. Highly recommended." - *Elizabeth Hunter, USA TODAY Bestselling Author of the Elemental Mysteries*

"Michelle M. Pillow brings us yet another hilariously touching story, this one set in the world of paranormal women's fiction, and you won't want to put it down. I know I didn't! Then again, she had me at séance." - *NY Times Bestselling Author Darynda Jones*

"When the past and the present merge...awesome author Michelle Pillow brings secrets from the grave and other things that go bump in the night into a fantastic story of second chances in the second act of life." - *Jana DeLeon, NY Times, USA TODAY, & Wall Street Journal Bestselling Author*

"Delightfully heartfelt and filled with emotion. Psychic powers, newly discovered magic, and a troublesome ex who comes back from the grave. Michelle M. Pillow delivers a wonderfully humorous start to a new paranormal women's fiction romance series." - *Robyn Peterman, NY Times and USA TODAY Bestselling Author*

"Second Chance Magic is full of heart and everything I love in a paranormal tale. Great friends, second chances, and physic powers... what's not to love?" - *Deanna Chase, NYT and USA Today Bestselling Author*

CHAPTER ONE

FREEWILD COVE, North Carolina

"Get that nonsense off your face."

Kari Grove shifted uncomfortably under the withering stare of her grandmother as she obeyed the command. She threaded the mask off her ears and dropped it to her lap. Even though the global pandemic was coming to an end, and she'd been vaccinated, Connie had not. The pandemic had made Kari hyper-aware of spreading germs, and with Connie sick, the mask felt like a no-brainer.

Connie continued to stare at her. Against her better judgment, Kari placed the mask on the nightstand.

"Only thieves and doctors wear masks," Connie continued, finally looking away. "A few people get a cold, and suddenly everyone is walking around like they're about to perform surgery and rob banks."

Connie Grove was eighty-five and still made her forty-year-old granddaughter feel like a disappointment, even now as she lay on her supposed deathbed. This was the sixth time Kari had been summoned to her grandmother's side, and she didn't believe it would be the last.

Nevertheless, how could she refuse to come? Connie was the only mother she'd ever known for all intents and purposes, and with that came a mix of emotions.

And drinking.

Sadly, it also came with a need for hard liquor to get through the visit.

Kari had never met her parents. They died the day she was born—her mother in childbirth, her father in grief. Without even holding his newborn daughter, the weak man walked out into traffic and was hit by a Chicago bus. At least, that's how her mother's parents always told the story. It was no secret they'd hated her father. They hadn't given Kari his last name, and they'd refused to talk about him.

Kari assumed they hated her mother for dumping a newborn on their laps. And, sometimes, she'd suspected it was because that newborn wasn't from the same "pristine" bloodlines as the rest of them—their phrasing not hers. Connie used to make excuses for Kari's unruly hair as if Groves were too good for curls.

Kari pushed a lock of hair out of her face and took a deep breath, steadying herself and doing everything she could to remain composed. Her grandparents had never been loving people. In fact, they were assholes.

That didn't mean Kari didn't love them in her own way. After her husband's death, Connie had become last of Kari's family. Good or bad, family meant something.

Didn't it?

"Connie, can I get you a drink?" Kari reached for the glass of water off the bedside table next to her discarded mask. She stood to offer the straw to her grandmother.

Connie waved her hand in dismissal and made a noise of disgust. "You were never a good listener, Lori."

"Connie, it's me, Kari. Lori was my mother." Kari returned to her seat and folded her hands in her lap.

"I know that," Connie snapped under her breath. Her legs worked restlessly on the bed, and she moaned. After a while, she continued, "I bet you drove that monstrosity onto my lawn again. You tore up the grass last time. I don't even want to contemplate what the neighbors think."

As a matter of fact, yes, Kari had parked her small RV out back again. Where else was she supposed to put her home?

"Mrs. Connie, isn't it nice your granddaughter is here?" Faith, the live-in nurse, walked into the room. The caretaker meant well and often tried to come to Kari's rescue. She'd gone downstairs to answer a knock on the front door.

"Who was at the—?" Kari tried to ask.

"Get me that. I'm parched." Connie waved her hand at the glass Kari had offered her moments before.

Faith automatically obeyed, keeping her tone low as she tried to soothe her irritated patient. She picked up the water and held the straw steady between two fingers as she brought it to Connie's mouth.

Faith was one of those people who had been born with a sunny disposition that even the darkest rain cloud couldn't seem to dampen. That, or she took some mighty powerful drugs to deal with Connie.

Kari wondered if Faith would share and resisted the urge to hum the tune for "Pass the Dutchie" under her breath.

"Who was at the door?" Kari asked once Connie had settled.

"A man is waiting downstairs to see you," Faith

answered quietly, nodding toward the bedroom door. "You go. I've got things under control up here."

Connie coughed and pushed the glass away. "I hope he's not like that one criminal you brought home. You broke your grandfather's heart. Though, *I* was hardly surprised. You always had the worst taste in men. It's no wonder you never married."

Wow. Connie was on a bitch roll today.

Kari took a deep breath and bore the criticism like she had since childhood.

Tommy Jenkins, her prom date, had been caught shoplifting T-bone steaks two years out of high school, long after they'd gone on that one date. That was a lifetime ago. Too bad there was no shelf life on mistakes in the Grove family. Anything you did wrong could be picked up and examined at any time.

Connie gave a weak laugh and turned to Faith. "Then she brought a drug dealer to Thanksgiving dinner. Eyes all glassy. Like we were too stupid to know what was going on. Did it just to prove a point. Lori didn't need our approval."

"I'm Kari. Paul took cold medicine. He wanted to stay home, but you insisted it was rude to cancel last minute because you had already planned the seating chart, and we couldn't have an empty place setting." Kari stood and walked to the bedroom door.

Why was she defending her old boyfriend? It was a useless argument that only went around in circles. She felt herself hitting her tolerance level and knew it was time to step away to regain her composure before she said something she'd regret.

"Listen to her sass me," Connie said to Faith. "She's always been ungrateful. Oh, and then there was that—*what's-her-name?*—odd girl with those funny little glasses who wore all black. You know who I'm talking about, don't you, Kari? She had a crush on you and—"

"Faith, I'll be right back." Kari closed the door behind her.

The wood barrier didn't stop the condemnations. Connie's muffled voice continued, "Always taking in strays, that one."

Kari's eyes drifted to a padlocked door across the hall as she listened. No matter how curious she was to see inside the storage room, she would never try to find the key. Connie had a lot of house rules. One being that no one was allowed beyond the locked door.

"You know she gave my late husband his heart attack, don't you?" Connie stated.

"Now, Mrs. Connie, you told me it was the cheeseburgers that gave him a heart attack," Faith admonished gently. "Don't go blaming that girl."

"Who do you think brought him the burgers?" Connie insisted.

Kari tried to ignore her grandmother's demeaning tone even as that age-old guilt surfaced like a brick inside her chest. No one could make her feel bad quite like Connie could. There was no point in debating the past. It wasn't an argument she would win.

Kari slipped next door to the guest room to take a quick swig of the flask she'd hidden under her pillow. The liquor burned, but she welcomed the sensation. Vodka had a nice way of not making her smell like a distillery. A little numbness would be just the thing to get her through the rest of the day.

Putting the flask away, Kari went to the top of the stairs and saw a man's legs in work pants standing by the front door. She had forgotten that a contractor was supposed to stop by for an estimate but was thankful for the reprieve. As she walked down the steps, more of him slowly came into view. If she wasn't so tired, she was sure she could have appreciated his gruff handsomeness—if only for the fact Connie would hate the idea of her dating a blue-collar worker with calluses on his hands. Or "the help," as Connie called everyone that she felt was beneath her.

Kari's eyes went to the man's ring finger and found

it empty. Would it be too strange to ask him to pretend to be her date long enough to meet Connie?

Kari tried not to laugh. Ah, the beautiful, subtle passive-aggressiveness of the idea.

"Mrs. Grove?"

A tiny shiver worked over her at the sound of his voice. She had not been expecting to actually feel attraction.

Kari shook off her childish impulses and paused on the bottom step. It took a moment for her to gather her thoughts and meet his handsome brown gaze. Dark hair framed his strong features, but what most caught her attention was his mouth.

The man smiled and made a point of looking around. "This is a beautiful home you have. Great bones. Large rooms. Original architectural details. They don't make them like this anymore."

It was a polite way of saying the décor was about forty years outdated.

The liquor did its job numbing her mind and it took her a moment to answer. She found herself staring at the strong line of his neck as he continued to inspect the foyer ceilings.

"It's not mine. It's my grandmother's," Kari answered, forcing her eyes to a splotch of dried paint on his t-shirt. It didn't help her concentration. "From what I've been told, it's an old family property, but it's been used as a rental house up until a few years ago when my grandmother moved back here."

Connie had moved into the two-story home after the death of her husband. Kari had never even heard her grandparents mention Freewild Cove until Kari got a change-of-address card in the mail. Ironically, Connie had called for a mailing address to send the card to instead of telling Kari on the phone like a normal person.

"Even so..." He nodded thoughtfully. "Is Mrs. Grove available?"

"She's not feeling well. I'm Kari Grove. I'm the one who called you. William, right?"

"Angel Molina, actually. I work with William Warrick. He had a family emergency and asked me to step in for him since you indicated you had an urgent situation."

"I hope everyone is all right," Kari answered.

"I believe so. His mother is having her gallbladder removed," Angel said. "I guess Bonnie has been ignoring the symptoms for a while now, and it has become serious enough to require immediate surgery. If you'd rather wait for him, I underst—"

"No, not at all. I appreciate you coming by on such short notice. I'm a little concerned about the ceiling in

9

here." Kari motioned for him to follow her into the living room.

The patterned yellow wallpaper made her dizzy just to walk into the room. The décor hadn't been touched since the nineteen-seventies. The carpet was a distinct shade of green with worn patterns and old stains long left to settle into darkened spots. The sofa and chair were a matching set and just as old and worn as the carpet. Someone had pushed a tattered coffee table close to the couch. Nicks and water spots lined the surface. This home seemed an odd choice for her fastidious grandmother. Maybe age had made the dust and stains impossible to see.

Kari stood close to the wide entryway and looked up. A long crack ran down a bow in the ceiling. She needlessly pointed toward it. "Not so great bones in here. My grandmother promised me the last five times I was here that she would get it looked at, but I think it's getting too bad to keep putting it off. I have to warn you, she won't be happy I called, but I can't leave it like this."

Angel gave a low whistle as he stepped past her into the room. "What happened?"

"I'm not sure." Kari followed him cautiously. "The last time I was here, it was a small bow. Now I feel like this side of the house will cave in at any moment."

Angel frowned as he walked the length of the room. "That's not natural wear and tear. What's above us? It looks like something is putting strain on the ceiling."

"I'm not sure," she repeated.

"We should take a look." Angel kept his gaze on the ceiling as he walked back toward the stairs.

"We can't." Kari followed him to the entryway and moved to stand between him and the staircase.

"I need to assess the damage if I—"

"Connie doesn't let anyone in that room. It's locked," Kari interrupted.

"Connie?"

"My grandmother," Kari clarified.

"Oh, well, I'm sure if we explain—"

"No. It's not possible. She's..." Kari glanced up the stairs. "I'm sorry, Mr. Molina. I keep cutting you off."

"Angel," he corrected. His kind smile acted like a warm beacon in her shitty day. He was probably just being nice and she was a complete mess.

"I'm sorry, Angel. I'm all over the place, but that's no excuse for rudeness. My grandmother's not well and not taking visitors. Is there something you can do from down here to make it safer? Anything? It doesn't have to be pretty."

"Brace it, maybe? It definitely won't be pretty."

Kari sighed. A slight headache settled behind her right eye. "She'll hate it, but I don't care what it looks like. She'll dislike the house falling out from under her even more."

Angel frowned. "I don't feel comfortable messing with the integrity of the room without seeing what we're working with, and without securing the express wishes of the homeowner. If you can get your gran—"

"That won't be possible," Kari insisted. She stared at the crack in the ceiling and couldn't look away. The headache became progressively worse, radiating behind both eyes and traveling from her temple down the side of her neck. "Not right now. I'm sorry."

"I can't recommend anyone going into the living room or the room above until you have it looked at. My gut tells me you shouldn't even be staying in the house." Angel frowned as if contemplating what he would do. "But, if you're going to be here, I can't in good conscience leave it like this. I can pick up a jack post if you'd like me to try to brace the ceiling, but it's a temporary solution and not the best one."

"Miss Kari," Faith called from upstairs, her voice soft and urgent at the same time. "You should come."

Kari blinked, prying her eyes from the crack. She glanced up the stairs and then at Angel. She felt a little nauseous. "Yes. Do that. Please. Anything."

"Miss Kari," Faith insisted, a little louder. "She's asking for you."

Kari took a backward step up. "Whatever you think is best, Mr.—uh, Angel."

She turned and rushed up the stairs. When she tried to brush past Faith in the hallway, her wrist bumped the door frame to the locked storage room. Pain shot up her arm.

"I'm sorry to interrupt, but she is very insistent that she talks to you. I think she wants to make peace," Faith said.

Kari's breath caught. Was this it? Connie's last moments? Was she finally going to say something nice? Try to connect to her? Say all the things she never said, like, *I love you, Kari?*

"If you need me, I'll be downstairs making her lunch," Faith said. "She needs something in her stomach before I give her meds."

The bedroom door hung open, and Kari pushed it out of her way. She felt a wave of dizziness and foreboding. There was nothing peaceful about the eyes that stared at her when she entered. She crossed the threshold into the bedroom.

"Connie? Faith said you had something to tell me," Kari prompted when the woman only continued to stare.

"You've always been a disappointment to me, Lori, since the day you were born," Connie said, her expression bordering on a snarl. The thread of hope she'd felt when Faith said Connie wanted to make peace burned up like a piece of tissue paper in a campfire.

I'm Kari.

She didn't bother to say the words out loud. It didn't matter.

"No matter what I did, nothing could fix what is broken in you. I bought you the best tutors, the most expensive classes, ballet lessons, horse-riding lessons, introduced you as a debutante into fine society, gave you the prettiest bedroom, and surrounded you with the prettiest things."

"You locked me in that room," Kari answered, not sure why she brought up her childhood punishments. Some memories were best left packed away.

"Little good it did," Connie countered.

A chill worked over her body under the coldness of Connie's stare. She felt her hands balling into fists as if they had a mind of her own. How much criticism did a person have to take in a lifetime?

I love you, Kari. Was that so hard to say?

"You should never have been born," Connie continued. "Of course you know that."

The headache became worse until Kari felt as if

the pounding radiated over her entire body. A mixture of sadness and rage filled her, taking her by surprise.

"I should have smothered you that first night in your crib and saved myself a lifetime of heartache and pain."

"Connie..." Kari tried to speak. Her hands shook as she came near the bed. She closed her eyes, clenching her fists. She needed her grandmother to stop talking. "Please. You don't mean that."

"Don't I?" Connie laughed. The sound was so cold and dismissive. "Have you ever known me not to say what I mean, Lori?"

"I'm Kari," she said, keeping her eyes closed.

"I know who you are," Connie snapped. "You killed your mother, Kari, and your father would rather kiss the front of a bus than—"

Kari felt a scream erupting from deep within as if forty years of ingesting a healthy dose of Connie's constant negativity had finally blossomed into something hateful and evil. She suppressed the scream, and that single act caused her throat to burn and her hands to shake. She wanted all of this to stop.

"Connie, I'm..." Kari's words trailed off as her eyes opened. She gripped a pillow tight, her fists balled around the thick stuffing. She didn't remember picking it up.

Connie's lifeless eyes stared past her toward the corner of the ceiling, her mouth slack.

In terror, Kari hugged the pillow to her chest and stepped back. The rage left her as quickly as it had flooded in. Her hands shook with panic and fear.

"Connie?" Kari whispered, willing her grand-mother to take a breath.

Oh, fuck. Oh, fuck. Oh, fuck.

What have I done?

"Soups ready," Faith announced from the doorway. "Are you having a nice chat, Mrs.—"

Kari turned. Her stricken expression stopped Faith from finishing.

"I..." Kari hugged the pillow tighter. "She..."

Faith rushed to set the food tray she carried on the nightstand and reached to touch Connie's neck. After a few seconds, she said, "I'm so sorry, dear. I didn't think we were that close to her time. I wouldn't have left you alone had I suspected."

Kari couldn't answer.

Oh, fuck.

Faith straightened Connie's head, closed her eyelids, and pushed her jaw closed before arranging her body to look more at peace.

"She's no longer in pain." Faith continued talking,

16

saying all the nice platitudes that people habitually expressed in these situations.

Kari still couldn't respond. She clutched the pillow tight as she backed out of the room.

Oh my God. What have I done?

CHAPTER TWO

COVE CEMETERY, *Two days later...*

For better or worse, she was the last living member of the Grove family.

Kari would have thought she'd feel lonelier at the notion, but the truth was she felt the same. The Groves had never felt like a family, not like those mildly dysfunctional but well-meaning units she'd grown up watching on television. The Groves were co-workers stuck in life's cubicles with crappy fluorescent lighting constantly humming in the background, only speaking because they were obligated to by circumstance. Sure, there were boring office birthday parties and the occasional work retreat, but for the most part, it was forced banality.

Family meant unity, connection, shared beliefs,

goals, something...anything. No matter how fucked up. What had her family shared?

Kari frowned, not seeing the gravesite even as she looked right at it.

The Groves shared disappointment and blame—in each other, in the world, in tattered dreams and personal failures. Clifford and Connie disliked the daughter they couldn't control and resented the grand-daughter they'd been required to raise. More honestly, Connie had disliked those things and Clifford disliked anything Connie told him to. They had been miserably negative people who could never be satisfied.

As Kari stood watching a priest who hadn't known her grandmother speak of the woman in glowing terms, thoughts whispered through her mind to drown him out.

Legacy. Duty. Disappointment. Blame. But not love.

The Groves didn't love each other. What other conclusion could Kari draw after forty years?

Even with all that personal baggage unpacking in her head to air out, Kari felt sadness as she peered at the edge of the hole. The woman had lived to be eighty-five. Connie would have called that a good run.

Kari gave a small laugh.

No, actually, Connie would be in the afterlife

hunting down her husband to brag that she beat him and lived longer.

Seeing the eyes of the priest on her, Kari covered her mouth and ducked her head. She licked her lips, almost desperate to taste a lingering hint of vodka on them. The flask in her purse called to her, but she held back. Sneaking a drink in the car was one thing. Getting loaded during a funeral sermon was quite another. Appearances mattered. Connie taught her that.

Faith stood beside her, rubbing her hand in small circles on Kari's back to comfort her. Every once in a while, she'd whisper things like, "She had a good long life."

Disappointment. Blame.

Kari kept her head down. She couldn't remember the other words she'd been thinking about a moment before.

She should be crying, not bemoaning her dysfunctional life.

The dull ache behind her eyes grew. Since Connie's death, the headache had lingered, and no amount of over-the-counter pain killers could tame it. Sure, the liquor probably wasn't helping, but how else was she supposed to get through this?

Blame.

Guilt churned inside her. The priest stared at her as he spoke.

I didn't do this. I couldn't do this. The thought had played on repeat in her head. *This wasn't me.*

Kari had kept waiting for the police to show up and arrest her. She'd expected the coroner to announce the death had been foul play before taking Connie away in that horrible black bag. She thought Faith might ask about the pillow sitting in the drier, still in its case. She'd been so sure the funeral home would have discovered something and stopped the funeral. Instead, they'd expedited it since there had been an opening in the schedule. Now, Kari expected the priest to declare she was going to hell.

None of that happened.

Surely that meant she had done nothing wrong. She had no memory of pressing the pillow to Connie's face. She could imagine it in vivid detail, but that wasn't the same thing.

Then why couldn't she shake the feeling? Why couldn't she get the image of Connie's dead face out of her head?

If only she had held her temper and waited a few minutes more before going down to talk to Angel. But in truth, Kari had been thankful for an excuse to leave the bedroom. That knowledge made the guilt worse. What kind of granddaughter preferred talking about structural damage with a stranger rather than sitting lovingly by the side of the woman who'd raised her?

If she had waited, Faith would have been in the room when Connie started rambling about smothering her as a baby. Nothing would have happened with Faith there.

Oh, but she had been so mad and hurt.

What really happened, though? Kari didn't believe herself capable of murder, so she probably had just grabbed the pillow and held it. Tight. While in a blinding rage.

Oh, fuck, what did I do?

Maybe it was like Faith said. It had been Connie's time.

Kari touched her purse, feeling the weight of the flask beneath the artificial leather.

"When I drop you off, do you want me to stay with you today, so you're not alone?" Faith asked, taking Kari by the elbow. The woman had offered to host a repast, but there was no one to invite to a reception.

Kari glanced up and realized the service was over. The priest looked at her with a strange mix of benevolence and pity. "No. I plan on going to sleep."

I plan on drinking myself to sleep.

A chill hit her face, and she touched her cheek in surprise to find tears wetting her skin.

"Thank you, Father," Faith said to the priest. Then to Kari, she added, "I'll stop by with food to check on you later."

"Thank you, but that won't be necessary. I'm not hungry. Some of the neighbors dropped off casseroles," Kari said. "They heard about Connie's passing and wanted to do something. Maybe I should have hosted a wake. Or repass. Repast? Repass? What did you call it again?" Kari rubbed the bridge of her nose. With each headache-pulse radiating over her temple, she found it more difficult to concentrate. "I don't know what I'm doing. I don't even know what I'm rambling on about right now. We don't have family. The neighbors were just being nice."

"Repast. I've changed my mind. I'm staying at the house with you tonight," Faith stated. "No arguments. You shouldn't be alone right now. There is a reason that people host receptions. Being around others and having something to focus on outside of yourself is good. Today, I'm your other."

Kari let Faith lead her over the lawn. She was too tired to protest. Having Connie's body in the ground gave her a sense of relief, which in turn made her feel ashamed.

Suddenly, Faith let go of her arm. "Meet me by the car. I'll be right back."

Kari automatically turned to watch Faith return to the gravesite. The movement resulted in a wave of lightheadedness that blurred her darkening vision. Her knees dropped, and she managed to catch herself before she fell to the ground.

Kari put her hand over her eyes to block the light as she tried to find her footing. She reached out to stop herself from tipping over. Her hand hit a hard object with a thud where there should have been only air.

Surprised, she jerked back and dropped the hand covering her face. She stood in the hallway of her grandmother's house on the second floor, beside the padlocked door to Connie's private storage room.

"*Wha—how?*" Kari glanced around in confusion. Her purse slid off her shoulder and landed on her foot. The flask fell out. She automatically moved to pick it up, only to stop.

Was this an alcoholic blackout? How else could she account for the missing time?

Fear gripped her, and she looked at her empty hands. Or was this like when she'd held the pillow?

"Faith?" Kari called, moving away from the door. Her foot bumped the flask and sent it sliding down the hall. "Faith, are you here? When did we get back from the cemetery?"

White light flashed behind her as she started down the staircase.

Fwap-fwap-fwap...

"What the...?" Kari frowned, turning toward the soft noise.

...fwap-fwap-fwap...

The light came from underneath the locked door.

"Faith?" Kari asked, wishing her voice was more assertive and at the same time too apprehensive about calling out. Her gaze went to the padlock. No one should be able to get into the room. Kari had yet to find the key.

Unless Connie had locked someone inside?

"She wouldn't." Kari went to the door. She felt a little dizzy as she grabbed her head.

Her grandmother had been a lot of things, but keeping someone barred in a room? This door had been padlocked since the first time Kari had been to the house.

Kari knocked on the door. "Hello?"

A memory tried to dig its way into her thoughts. Kari jiggled the door handle, trying to peek through the seam where the door met the wall. Light managed to make it through, but she couldn't see into the room.

Her breath bounced off the door to hit her in the face. The tickle became a blurry recollection. She'd been like this before, her face pressed to a door, desperate to see around the sliver of wood blocking her view, trying to pull the air into her lungs from the other side.

...fwap-fwap-fwap...

Connie *would* lock someone in a room. In fact, she had.

"Connie, please tell me you didn't trap a child in here."

Kari inhaled sharply to fill her lungs as she pulled away from the wood. A sense of panic filled her chest. Her heart beat in heavy thumps, which triggered a pounding in her ears. She smacked the flat of her hand against the door. "Hello? Is someone in there?"

Liquor caused her thoughts to swim. She rattled at the knob again. Why was this room locked? Who could be inside?

This made no sense.

Every horror movie she'd ever seen didn't provide a good answer to that question.

...fwap-fwap-fwap...

Kari glanced around, wondering where Connie would have hidden the key. Then, realizing her grandmother wasn't there to stop her and the house as good as belonged to her, she yelled, "Stand away from the door. I'm coming in!"

Kari slammed her shoulder into the door to try to force it open. The screws holding the padlocked latch lifted from the frame. She struck it again, wrenching its tight hold. On the third strike, the wood splintered, and she fell into the room. Dust swirled under the sudden rush of her movement.

...fwap-fwap-fwap...

Heavy curtains blocked the sunlight, held in place by a cabinet shoved against the window. The source of the flashing light and steady sound came from behind a stack of old boxes in the center of the room. Frayed edges and bent cardboard created a strange cubicle. Stacks of magazines and yellowed newspapers fortified the edges. Bunches of dried flowers tied with ribbons had been placed on top of the boxes as if crowning the hoarder's stash.

A layer of dust covered every surface. Shuffling footsteps had crossed the wood floor at one time, but it appeared as if years had passed by the amount of dust filling the imprints. Kari slid her foot on the ground, comparing the print her foot left behind.

...fwap-fwap-fwap...

"Hello?" Kari coughed and swatted her hands

through the air in a vain attempt to clear the dust. All the motion did was churn the particles.

...fwap-fwap-fwap...

"What the hell, Connie?" Kari whispered. Sheets hung over furniture like misshapen ghosts, gathered in a corner around a seamstress mannequin. There were steamer trunks, stacked plastic containers, and a pile of creepy old dolls with ratted hair and broken limbs. "No wonder the living room ceiling is about to cave in."

Too much flask and not enough food made Kari's head spin.

Kari glanced over her shoulder at the open door before slowly making her way around the boxes. The floor groaned beneath her weight as if each extra pound might be the one to send it crashing through to below. She stepped over an orange extension cord snaking across the floor. Her unsteady steps followed the old, shuffled footprints, disturbing the dust.

...fwap-fwap-fwap...

Someone had set up a projector in the small alcove of boxes. Movement caught her eye. An image shone on the wrinkles of the falling sheet that had been pinned up for a screen. Kari instantly recognized her mother as a teenager, not that her mother had made it out of her teen years.

What she didn't recognize was the film. Why hadn't her grandmother shown this to her?

Beyond the steady *fwap* of the projector, the room was silent. Lori twirled in fast circles, only to stop and point to the side. She appeared to laugh as her lips moved. Kari inched closer but couldn't make out what her mother had said.

Her mother had been a true beauty, with the kind of smile that would have enthralled people.

Kari's grandmother had never been an easy woman to know. In some ways, being raised by Connie had made Kari feel closer to her mother. She always wondered if their childhoods had been the same. Had the constant need to be perfect nagged at her mother until it infected her entire life? Was Lori's smile a mask, hiding something more? Was that why she ran off to Chicago to get married?

Suddenly, Lori's smile faded. It felt as if her mother looked directly at her as she mouthed the word, "Look."

Kari's eyes blurred with tears. She followed her mother's pointed finger with her gaze. On the floor, wedged between two boxes, a tiny glint of metal caught her attention. She leaned closer to find a gold wedding band. The second that Kari's fingers made contact, heat washed over her body. She wiggled the ring free.

...fwap-fwap-fw—

The projected image stopped flickering, and a blast of orange lit the boxed alcove. The heat intensified. Kari turned, falling back against the cardboard barrier as the projector caught fire. The film melted, curling through the air like a flaming snake to ignite a nearby box.

Kari tried to dart past the projector. The fire snake lunged for her, blocking her path. The flames became hotter.

Trapped, she screamed, "Help! Faith!"

Kari thrust her shoulder into the wall of boxes. She dug her feet into the floor as she pressed against the heavy weight to knock them over.

"Faith! Are you here?" Kari yelled. The box wall gave way, and she tumbled over with them in her effort to escape.

A loud crack sounded as the boxes struck the floor. A little bounce knocked the air from her lungs and jarred her shoulder, but she didn't stop falling. Wood scraped her arm and thumped her head. Her limbs flailed as she passed through the floor.

"Oh my God," a woman screamed.

Kari landed on a pile of debris. She was unable to focus as movement came from above.

"Heather, grab her," another voice ordered.

Hands took hold of her arms and dragged her roughly from the pile seconds before another crash sounded.

"Are you all right?" the first woman asked. Kari saw a swish of reddish-blonde hair and felt someone touching her legs.

"Fire! Angel, bring the extinguisher," yet a third woman ordered, followed by running footsteps.

Dark brown eyes came into focus as a woman leaned over her. "We need to get you out of here. Can you move?"

Kari gasped for breath. As the shock of the fall subsided, pain radiated through her body. Her arm throbbed, and a sharp ache pulsed on top of her head.

"My name is Vivien," the dark-eyed woman stated, her words slow. "Can you tell me your name?"

Kari opened her mouth but only managed to wheeze. The ceiling creaked, and more debris fell from above.

"Lorna, we need to get her to safety," Vivien said. "Can we move her?"

"I think she might've broken her leg," the blonde touching her calf said. "I can't tell. We shouldn't move her. I don't think I can fix paralysis if her neck is injured."

"Heather? How's it looking up there?" Vivien yelled.

"Stay back," the woman upstairs hollered in return.

"Give me some of her pain," Vivien told Lorna. "Start with the head, so she can tell us what happened."

Shouts came from upstairs, and a fine white mist showered down from the hole in the ceiling onto the pile of box rubble. Kari focused her confused attention on it, not sure what she was hearing.

"Careful, Angel!" Heather warned. A series of thuds and crashes sounded.

"Keep back. I see it," Angel replied.

Lorna placed a hand on Kari's forehead. Her skin tingled at the contact. The woman had a sympathetic expression. "Don't worry. We're going to take care of you."

"Crap. I was right. We had to come. Look." Vivien lifted Kari's hand. The ring she'd found between the boxes was halfway down her pointer finger. "She has a ring."

"We got the fire out!" Heather yelled.

Lorna and Vivien didn't answer.

"Do you think..." Lorna pulled back her hand, and the tingling stopped. She leaned to look up into the hole. "Heather, careful up there. We don't know what this is. She has a ring!"

"What?" Heather looked as if she was on her hands and knees as she leaned over to peer down the hole at them.

"Ring!" Vivien repeated.

"Not another one. Dammit, Julia," Heather muttered as she disappeared from view.

Heavy footsteps came down the stairs and ran out the front door.

"Angel is grabbing a jack so that we can brace the floor. There's a lot of weight shoved up there." Heather appeared over Kari. "How is she?"

"I..." Kari tried to answer.

Lorna put one hand back on Kari's head and then reached to place her free hand over Vivien's. The tingling started again, and the pain lessened.

Kari's vision improved while the white of Vivien's left eye filled with red, and she groaned. "Whoa, someone's been drinking. I wasn't ready for the buzz."

"She needs a hospital," Lorna stated. "There is only so much I can do."

"I called 911," Heather said. As if supporting the statement, the distant sound of sirens came from outside. "Give me some of her pain."

Heather reached toward Lorna but pulled back as Angel entered carrying a long metal pole.

He glanced down at Kari in worry. "Is she going to be all right?"

"Oh, yeah," Lorna said, the words unconvincing. "She's going to be fine."

Vivien just held her head and moaned.

"I swear I'm not trying to feel you up." Lorna placed her tingling hands on Kari's upper chest. The women's expression slowly changed, and her brow furrowed as if she were in pain.

The ache in Kari's back began to ease.

"In here," Heather directed.

Paramedics arrived with a stretcher.

"I think we got the fire out," Heather continued as a couple of firefighters followed her direction upstairs. "Careful of the floor."

"I'm fine," Kari tried to say as the two EMTs shooed Vivien and Lorna back.

"What happened?" The man's embroidered name danced before her gaze. Perry. "Another Glenn-demon?"

"A Glenn-what?" his partner asked, setting down her medic bag.

"Not funny," Vivien groaned, holding her head.

"She fell..." Lorna began to explain.

"Through that?" Perry asked in surprise.

Kari tried to sit up. She didn't like all these people staring at her and touching her. She felt trapped.

"Try not to move," Perry ordered.

"My name is Florence. Can you tell me your name?" the female EMT demanded more than asked.

"Kari," she managed, trying to move her limbs to assess the damage from the fall for herself.

"Kari, I need you to lie still for me." Florence inhaled through her nose as she slipped a stiff collar around Kari's neck to stabilize it. "Have you been drinking?"

"She fell through the ceiling," Lorna interrupted. "We pulled her out of danger, but we didn't want to do more damage. I think she might have broken her leg."

"She appears stable enough to transport. I'll get the back board and stretcher." Perry stood up and left.

Kari heard the firefighters talking through the hole in the ceiling.

"We need to get everyone out of here until we can secure the scene," a man ordered.

Angel passed by, giving her a worried look as he went back outside.

"Did you fall?" Florence asked Vivien.

"A box fell on me," Vivien lied.

Kari had seen Vivien's eye turn red when Lorna

touched both of them. At the same time, the pain in her head had eased.

But that hardly made sense.

"It fell on all of us," Vivien said with a nod at Lorna. "But we'll be fine."

"Yes, check Kari first," Lorna said. "My back is just a little sore."

"You're all very lucky." Florence lifted a penlight to examine Vivien's eyes more closely.

Kari stared past her toward the broken ceiling. That didn't feel lucky. The giant hole felt like a metaphor for her day—cracked and damaged. Hell, it felt like a metaphor for her life.

What did it matter? What did any of this matter?

Maybe I deserve this, she thought.

A tear slid down her cheek, and she closed her eyes. This day needed to end.

"All three of you need to go to the hospital to get checked out," Florence ordered, leaving no room for argument.

"I can drive Viv and Lorna. We'll follow you," Heather answered, before yelling toward the door, "Angel, can you take care of things here?"

Kari opened her eyes and reached for Vivien. She grabbed her arm, stopping her when she would follow Heather. "Wait. What's a Glenn-demon?"

Vivien smirked. "Lorna's asshole ex-husband. I'll tell you about it later. Now that story could fill an entire book."

"Yeah, and we can call it the new Necronomicon," Lorna muttered.

Perry returned with the stretcher.

"Here's your ride," Florence said. "Time to go."

CHAPTER THREE

FREEWILD COVE HOSPITAL

"You're looking better. A little less like a crash test dummy."

Vivien strode into Kari's hospital room in a hospital gown like she walked down a runway. Even with the white of her eye turned red, she was unmistakably beautiful. It wasn't just her face, but the way she carried herself. Beauty was a natural side effect of confidence.

Vivien gave a small turn to show off the fact she wore two gowns—a second one like a robe to keep her ass from hanging out. "Apparently, my outfit had too many sparkly bits for the CAT scan, so they stole my clothes."

Kari placed her half-eaten supper of green gelatin on the bedside table. "Do we...? Were you...?"

"Oh, no. The fall caused you to forget how to form whole sentences," Vivien teased with a wink.

Kari chuckled as she felt the bump on her head. The doctor said she was fortunate. She assumed he didn't know the whole story.

"Go ahead." Vivien smiled. "Ask what you're going to ask."

"What were you doing in Connie's house?" Kari dropped her hand in her lap. They'd given her two IV bags' worth of fluids, which had stopped the hangover she should have been suffering. It also finally eased the headache that had plagued her for days.

"Lorna made you cinnamon rolls. When Angel mentioned to William—who is Heather's brother and also dating Lorna—what had happened while he was at your house to give an estimate, we wanted to do something for you. We were dropping them off to give our condolences." Vivien lightly tapped the side of Kari's leg to get her to move over a little as she sat at the end of the hospital bed. "No cast?"

"Not broken." Kari pulled the thin hospital blanket aside to give a peek of her leg, showing a long line of dark stitches. "They had to stitch up my calf."

"Should make for a cool scar and decent bar story,"

Vivien said. "It's a good thing we heard you scream and let ourselves in, or you'd be trapped under an abnormally large pile of boxes. What were you doing up there? Smoking doobies inside your box fort?"

"Why do you automatically assume I was doing drugs?" Kari pulled the blanket back over her leg.

"When Lorna transferred your..." Vivien touched her temple close to her red eye. "Never mind. Bad joke. So what were you doing up there?"

Kari looked at her pointer finger to where she still wore the ring. A delicate pattern had been carved along the jewelry's edge. At the time, she would have sworn her mother showed it to her. Now sober, she knew that wasn't possible. It was simply a lost item in a room full of junk. "I found an old projector, and I was watching a movie of my mother. I think Connie used the room for storage. I don't know what all she kept in there."

"Connie? I thought she was your grandma?" Vivien smiled, and her eyes looked genuinely interested in the answer.

"She is."

"And you call her Connie?"

Kari gave a slight shrug. "She insisted."

"Was she a cold fish, or did she have a problem with people thinking she was old?" Vivien asked.

"Viv!" Heather appeared in the doorway. She frowned at her friend. "You can't ask people things like that. Not after the day she's had."

"It's all right." Kari wasn't sure why these women were in her room, but she found herself glad for the company. "Probably both reasons are true."

"See," Vivien said to Heather. "I knew she'd be fine with it. She's stronger than she looks."

At that, Kari laughed. "I'm not so sure about that."

"I'm very sorry to hear about your," Heather shared a look with Vivien, "Connie. She and my grandma Julia were friends when they were younger. Julia Warrick?"

"Connie never mentioned her." Kari's leg throbbed along the stitches. She sat up, leaning to the side to adjust her position. "Does Julia live around here? The funeral home helped me put a notice in the paper, but I didn't know to inform anyone directly."

"Julia passed away years ago." Vivien shared another strange look with Heather as if they communicated without words.

"Weren't the two of you close?" Heather asked.

Kari looked from one woman to the other. Close? No, she and Connie had not been close.

Kari gripped the thin blanket covering her lap as

the memory of Connie's face in that last moment tried to cloud her mind. She took a deep breath.

"In a way, I guess we were." Kari carefully chose her words. "She and my grandfather raised me after my mother died giving birth to me. Well, she was there when I was raised. The nannies did most of the work. Connie wasn't what you would call a sharer. She didn't talk about things or people. I didn't even know there was a family home in a town called Freewild Cove until after she moved back here. I had been planning on visiting her in Illinois when she called to tell me she'd moved."

To herself, Kari corrected, *Well, technically, she called to get my mailing address so that she could notify me that she'd moved by a change-of-address card.*

There was no need to get into the details of all that.

"She doesn't want to talk about this." Vivien nodded as if she could read Kari's thoughts.

Thankfully, that was impossible. Kari didn't want anyone seeing what was in her head.

"I'm sorry," Vivien continued. "You've had a rough road. Perfection isn't attainable, and yet some still strive to force it from others."

"Okay?" Kari wasn't sure what Vivien meant by that.

"What she means to say is we're sorry for your

loss." Heather pulled on Vivien's arm to make her stand from the bed. "We'll leave you be, but please let us know if you need anything. Call the Warrick Theater downtown. Or the number you have for William. We're easy enough to track down."

"Wait, William, your brother. He couldn't make our meeting because of your mother. Angel said she was having emergency surgery. How is she?" Kari asked.

Heather appeared surprised by the question. "Oh, yeah, thanks, she's doing better now. I just came from checking in on her. She'd been ignoring back pains for months, thinking she strained a muscle. Turns out it was referred pain from her gallbladder. Another two or three days, and it would have been really bad news."

"We'll stop by again on our way out. Just as soon as I find where that nurse stashed my clothes." Vivien gave Kari a little wave as they started to leave.

Kari's finger tingled. She tugged at the ring, but it was stuck on her hand. Both Vivien and Heather grabbed their own hands and turned to look at her. Their eyes focused on where she pulled on the jewelry.

"I told you," Vivien stated. "We have another one."

Heather took a deep breath and appeared resigned. She came back into the room. "Kari, this might be an odd question, but has anything strange happened to you lately?"

She thought of the pillow and swallowed nervously.

"You mean like falling through the living room ceiling?" Kari asked.

"Stranger than that," Vivien said. "Maybe unexplainable?"

"Like the three of you showing up when you did?" The tingling in her hand became more substantial, and Kari rubbed her palm. "I hit my head pretty hard when I landed, but for a second, it looked like—Lorna, was it? —somehow caused your eye to turn red when she touched you."

"Yes." Vivien nodded. "Things like that."

Kari refused to think of Connie. Instead, she thought of the lost time between the cemetery and the house. She thought of the projector running in a locked room. Both incidents seemed strange, but they had to have a logical explanation. She was in no condition to think of what that might be.

"No," she lied. "It's been a terrible, long day, at the end of a very long, lousy week."

On the journey of a very long, bad life.

Connie was gone. Kari had no family left. She'd soon officially inherit a broken house she didn't want in a town she could barely find on a map. What should she do now?

Besides feeling sorry for herself, of course.

A tear slipped down her cheek, and she brushed it away. "Thank you for checking on me. And for saving me. And for the cinnamon rolls. But I think I need to sleep now."

"Of course." Vivien nodded.

"Let's go find Lorna," Heather said.

"Call us," Vivien insisted. "If you need anything."

Kari nodded and closed her eyes. She listened to the women leave. The door closed behind them.

Kari didn't want to be here. She hated hospitals—the smell of sickness and disinfectants and the over-priced tissues that cost thirty dollars apiece. Being a freelance graphic artist living in an RV didn't usually come with viable health care options.

I guess money isn't a concern now.

Connie wasn't exactly the type to leave her money to charity. She had too much pride in the family name to leave a member poor.

Kari took a deep breath.

"Oh, hey, I didn't hear you come back." Angel was the last person she expected to visit her in the hospital.

Kari opened her eyes to find him standing over her.

She shivered and her heartbeat quickened. "Mr. Molina?"

"Angel," he corrected. He leaned back and glanced around in confusion. "Do you need help?"

Kari realized she lay in the middle of the hallway in Connie's house. She gasped, sitting up. The sudden movement jarred her sore body. How in the hell did she get here?

"You're bleeding." Angel gestured at her arm. He seemed concerned by didn't comment on the incredibly odd scene circumstances. "Do you need me to call someone? An ambulance?"

Kari checked where the IV had been in her hand. It looked as if it had been yanked out. She swiped the dotting blood against her leg, only to realize she wore the hospital gown and her naked ass pressed against the floor.

She bunched the gown behind her as she stood, keeping her back to the wall. "They, uh, cut my clothes, and I had to wear..."

The lie was weak, and he didn't look as if he believed her anyway. She stood, staring at him for a long moment. His nearness made her a little nervous, mostly because she was attracted to him and wasn't currently making a very good impression. The thin material of the gown probably didn't leave much to the imagination, especially when she pulled the flaps closed behind her, and it molded against her body. His eyes started to travel down, but he caught himself and returned his gaze to her face. She became aware of the fact they were probably alone in the house.

Suddenly, he smiled. "If you wanted to escape from a hospital, that's your business. Can't say I care for doctors either."

The statement was oddly understanding considering the circumstances. The man radiated kindness. Not necessarily charisma and charm, or some fake social nicety, but genuine, pure compassion. After a lifetime of Connie, Kari knew how to spot the negativity in people. Angel didn't appear to have any.

"You won't find me judging you," Angel continued. "Where my family is from, my grandpa is famous for running out during a procedure without his pants, screaming that the doctor tried to unwrap his package. To hear my grandma tell it, he traumatized a couple of nuns and made two nurses quit. They found him a few hours later at a local bar. Still pants-less."

Kari laughed despite her situation. She kept her back toward the hallway wall as she inched past him. Stiff muscles reminded her of what had happened. The stitched wound on her leg ached each time she put weight on that foot. "What was the procedure?"

"My grandma had signed him up for a vasectomy and told him it was a regular checkup." Angel grinned. "I think she hoped he wouldn't catch on until it was too late."

"That can't be a real story." Kari made it past him and quickly backed her way toward the stairs, careful to keep her butt from view.

"All true. They had twelve children, and my *abuela* was not about to add unlucky number thirteen." He grinned as he turned to go into the living room.

"What are you doing here?" Kari paused on the first step and leaned to watch him. He'd swept the debris into a pile and moved the fallen boxes out of the way of the hole.

"Bracing the ceiling to steady things upstairs, so we can start moving furniture out of the room for repairs." Angel studied her when she didn't readily speak. "No charge if that's what you're worried about. I couldn't leave you like this, especially knowing what you're going through."

"You can't do that. I want you to charge me. No one should work for free. Please do what you need to do to fix it," she answered. What did it matter? As soon as the lawyer executed the will, she'd have more money than she needed. If it turned her into her embittered grandparents, she didn't want any of the family fortunes. "Is it safe to be upstairs? I need a change of clothes."

Angel gestured toward her. "Just stay on that side of the house. But I wouldn't recommend living here until we can do a full inspection. Better safe than sorry."

Kari nodded. "It's fine. I can stay in my RV."

She preferred that anyway.

As she walked up the stairs, watching her bare feet against the wood, she realized she didn't care if the house collapsed around her. Exhaustion filled each breath. Sore muscles and joints protested every movement. She ignored Connie's closed door, not wanting to think about those last moments. Instead, she paused near the broken frame of the once-locked storage room.

The smell of burnt cardboard lingered in the air. Light came from the hole in the floor, revealing the floating dust particles. Some of the boxes had been pushed aside, and firefighters' boot prints created chaos in the dust. The sheet where her mother's image had been hours before was gone, and only the scorched projector remained.

Tingles radiated from the ring. This time when she tugged at it, the jewelry slid off her finger.

"It might get a little loud," Angel called.

"Do what you have to," Kari answered. "Thank you!"

She shuffled toward the guest bedroom where she'd been staying. Connie hated that Kari lived in a place with wheels and had refused to let her granddaughter sleep on the lawn. Not that it mattered what Connie thought now.

Kari placed the ring on the night table and fell into bed without bothering to put on clothes. The task of walking back downstairs felt impossible. The only thing she cared about right now was sleep.

CHAPTER FOUR

KARI AWOKE TO A LOUD, rhythmic banging. At first, she thought the pounding was in her head, the sharp pulse there to remind her that she'd had one too many drinks the night before. She had always joked to herself that Connie had a way of inducing alcoholism in others. Numbness made the woman's sharp words bearable.

No, not a hangover. Hammer.

Headache. Shut up, hammer.

Connie is dead. I am alone.

What did I do?

Boom. Boom. Boom.

Ugh, why is there a friggin' hammer?

Kari opened her eyes at the scattered thoughts and was welcomed by the popcorn texture on the ceiling.

Tiny flecks of silver dotted the bumpy surface. It reminded her of stars against a dingy white sky. The view was a poor comparison to waking up in the middle of nature surrounded by peace.

This wasn't home. She had no connection to this fragment of her family's past or to the town of Freewild Cove. The location looked like a thousand different small towns she'd driven through over the years. At most, she'd stop for gas and a hamburger before moving on down the road.

She couldn't move on. Not yet.

"I don't want to do today," she whispered.

The ceiling held no answers. It didn't even have the decency to cave in and take the option away from her.

Kari's wants rarely mattered in Connie's world. Thank you cards needed to be written for the casseroles. The lawyer needed her to sign papers and go over the estate paperwork. Evidently, people were hard at work fixing the broken old house...with a really loud hammer.

What would happen if she walked away from it all? Just got into her mobile home and drove away from South Carolina and never looked back? It's not like anyone could make her pack up Connie's belongings and take responsibility for old furniture and ugly, faded carpet. Eventually, the banks, or tax authorities, or vagrants would come in and just take what they wanted. Indeed people had the choice to walk away and not accept the responsibility.

As tempting as it sounded, Kari knew she didn't have it in her. Someone had to pay the workers. Someone had to close the house. Someone needed to go through the belongings. Maybe she'd discover more about her parents. The projector film was clearly lost in the fire, but Connie might have hidden other movies within the walls of the box fort.

The nerves in her hand buzzed, and she looked down to see she wore the ring she'd found. Kari glanced at the night table; sure she'd taken the jewelry off. Or maybe she'd dreamed of doing it.

Maybe all this was a dream.

It was hard to know what was real anymore.

There had to be a compromise between familial duty and what she wanted to do. Maybe she could leave and have the lawyer email her whatever information he had for her. Or she could call him and say she didn't want it and to make sure the estate paid the workers downstairs. Or to turn it into a trust for stray cats.

Connie would hate the cat idea. Kari kind of loved it.

Who was she kidding? As much as she wanted to shirk her responsibilities, she knew she couldn't. The childhood guilt of family obligation ran deep. There were others Connie needed to pay besides the contractor, like Faith, who didn't deserve to be left high and dry by Kari's selfishness. Those checks wouldn't write themselves.

"Think positive. Just because you were raised in negativity doesn't mean you have to be negative." Kari had first given herself this same pep talk in high school after a friend called her out on her self-deprecating humor.

All right. Positives.

Having money in the bank would be nice for a change.

When her RV broke down, she wouldn't be stuck in Colorado waitressing to save enough cash to fix it...again.

She wouldn't have to take every graphic art job that came her way. Or discount it beyond a reasonable amount because she was desperate for work.

She might discover something about her past.

Kari sat on the edge of the bed in her hospital gown. Though sore, thankfully her body didn't hurt as much as the night before. Inflamed tissue surrounded the dark stitches on her calf. The doctor had said something about taking it easy for a few days. He'd also said something about antibiotics, but she'd left the hospital before she could get the prescriptions.

Left the hospital? So that was what she called blacking out and waking up on the hallway floor?

The tingling in her hand intensified. A softer knock beneath the incessant hammering drew her attention toward the closed door.

"Kari? Are you awake?" a voice called.

Kari frowned and went to peek out of the room while hiding her outfit behind the door.

Heather stood holding a takeout coffee. "Thought I'd bring you breakfast." She handed the coffee through the cracked door. "How are you?"

Kari took a sip of the hot coffee and gave a little moan of appreciation.

A man's heavy footsteps came up the stairs, and a shout sounded from below. Kari opened the door wider and waved the woman inside before closing them in.

Heather set a plastic bag on the bed and then eyed the hospital gown. "I heard you pulled a hospital Houdini."

"What's for breakfast?" Kari asked to change the subject. She had no explanation for how she got home.

"Coffee." Heather gestured to the cup before touching the plastic bag. "These are your things from the hospital. Lorna washed your clothes for you. She's a mother hen. She can't help herself."

"That was nice of her." Kari removed the lid from the cup and took another drink.

"Last night, when I checked in to see if Angel needed help with the ceiling, he mentioned you were home. I called Vivien, and she made sure the hospital discharged you out of their system and didn't call the police to report you missing. She told them what you were going through with the funeral, and they were understanding about it." Heather gave a small laugh. "Vivien has a way of convincing people to do what she wants."

"Oh, um, thank you. I didn't even think about them calling the police to find me."

"We're supposed to make sure you go in this week for a checkup." Heather lifted the plastic bag, only to drop it again. "We picked up your antibiotics. There is a prescription for painkillers. You'll need to bring your ID down to the pharmacist to get it filled. He'll want to do a consultation. Henry's son has struggled with opioid abuse, so he's very particular about giving any out."

"I think I'll be all right without them." Kari looked at her stolen gown. "I guess I should get this back to the hospital."

Heather gave a small, dismissing wave. "They probably won't notice."

"All the same." Kari pulled the gown closed behind her and held it in a fist as she went to the dresser.

"I can drop it off when I pick up my mom later to give her a ride home," Heather offered. She pulled a small notebook and pen from the front pocket of her flannel shirt and jotted down a quick note. "I'm sure you have enough to do."

"That would be great, thank you." Kari took a pair of loose slacks and a suit jacket out of the drawer, then reached for a t-shirt to go under it. Connie would have hated the choice. "Can I ask you something?"

"You don't need to ask permission to ask me something," Heather said. "Just ask."

"Why are you guys being so nice to me? You don't know me. It doesn't sound like you knew Connie." Kari stopped short of pointing out her grandmother wasn't exactly in the business of making friends.

"Would you rather we throw rotten tomatoes at your front door?" Heather offered with a small laugh.

"I'm not ungrateful. I just... I guess..." Kari took a deep breath. "It's unexpected. I'm overwhelmed, and it's unexpected."

Heather nodded, her smile dropping some. She

seemed to choose her words carefully. "We understand what you're going through."

"The funeral?" Kari tried to discern what the woman meant.

"That, yes, and well, to be honest, Viv is much better at explaining these kinds of things than I am, but yes, we understand loss. We understand feeling alone." Heather twisted the ring on her finger. "We understand what it is to be women of our ages balancing on the edge of change. So we're here. To help. If you want it."

"Change? You think I'm in menopause?" Kari scrunched up her nose and automatically glanced into the mirror. She did look worn. Her curly hair seemed a little more unruly than normal.

Heather shook her head. "I mean general, unexpected life changes."

Kari's hand felt numb, and she gave it a couple of hard flicks to get rid of the sensation. "That's very kind of you. Thank you."

"It takes some getting used to." Heather nodded toward Kari's hand before averting her gaze as she dressed.

"I'm a little slow on the uptake today. What are you trying to say?" Kari pulled on underwear and slacks beneath the hospital gown, careful not to bump the stitches.

"I'm saying I know the reason you keep rubbing your hand and why you probably feel like there are goosebumps on your scalp whenever we're near you. We know some kind of strangeness must have occurred before you fell through the floor last night. And I might be able to shed some light on anything unexplained that's happening to you." Heather rubbed her eye with the side of her finger. "There is no easy way of saying this. That ring you found came from my grandma Julia."

"Oh?" Kari looked at the band. "Does your family want it back? I didn't know."

Heather kept her attention toward the wall. "No, we won't want it back."

Kari slipped off the gown and threaded her arms through a bra before pulling on a t-shirt. It only mildly registered that she was getting dressed with a stranger in the room, but it didn't bother her. Years of showering at campsites had desensitized her to such modesties.

"If you found the ring, Julia wants you to have it." Heather continued to look away.

Kari refrained from answering the strange comment.

"You're going to think I'm a nutcase, but I'm just

going to say it. The ring is magical. It came to you because you're coming into your personal magic. Strange things and probably scary things are going to start happening to you. It might be ghosts, or demons, or ex-husbands, or I don't know..."

Heather was right. She did sound like a nutcase.

Kari stood, stunned, unsure how to respond. Ghosts? Demons? Did she laugh? Did she run? Did she scream? Did she confess she'd had a couple of blackouts, which most likely were caused by drinking on an empty stomach at a funeral?

Did she say she blacked out by Connie's deathbed?

"Um, I've never been married," she finally managed.

Kari found herself glancing around the room for her grandmother's ghost. That was the last thing she needed, Connie the not-so-friendly spirit floating around silently judging her. Or worse. What if Kari had done something to her? Would she come for revenge?

"Great, so we can check ex-husband off the list." Heather tried to laugh, but the sound was weak. "I'm actually glad. The last ex we dealt with was a doozy."

"I..." Kari let loose a long breath. "I'm sorry I can't visit longer. I have to meet the lawyer and sign some papers. And maybe find a real estate agent about what to do with this house."

"I understand. I'll go." Heather went toward the bedroom door and opened it. The sound of construction became louder. "When it starts, call us. Whatever it is, we'll believe you."

That sounded ominous.

Kari slowly pulled on her shoes and waited in the room to give Heather time to leave.

"I can't deal with weird today," she whispered. Then, getting chills at the idea of ghosts, she glanced around. "And don't you dare try to haunt me, Connie, or I'll make Tommy Jenkins my prison pen pal."

A loud door slam answered her threat, startling Kari. Shouts from below indicated the workers were responsible.

"I'm sorry, Connie," Kari whispered, shaking as she amended her tone from earlier. "Please don't haunt me."

Kari found her purse by the bedroom door on the floor. She must have dropped it in the hall. The flask was underneath it. She put the liquor on the bedroom nightstand and carried the purse.

A couple of men came from the damaged storage room wearing masks. They lugged a dresser down the stairs.

"Ma'am," one of them nodded at her as they passed.

She gave a weak wave. "Hi."

Kari peeked into the storage room. Light came from the hole in the floor. Most of the furniture and the creepy sewing mannequin were cleared out. A wall of boxes remained on the far side of the damaged projector, but several had been removed. The air still smelled of burnt cardboard and dust.

The sound of Faith's soft humming drew her to Connie's bedroom door. The woman smiled as she folded laundry. Several of the medical supplies that had sat by the bed had been packed into boxes.

"There you are." Faith placed the shirt she'd been folding on the table. "You had me worried when I couldn't find you after the funeral, and then when I came by the house, and they told me you'd had an accident."

"I was so tired. I got another ride," Kari lied. "I'm sorry. I didn't mean for you to worry."

"You're safe. That's all that matters." Faith went back to folding.

"I can take care of all of this," Kari offered. "You don't have to clean up."

"You have plenty on your plate today, Miss Kari," Faith said. "I got this."

Kari thanked her. For as bitter of a woman as Connie had been in life, there were a lot of nice people around for her death. She thought of Heather and her ghosts. Well, nice and weird.

"Oh, here," Faith said when Kari was halfway down the steps. She jingled then tossed a set of keys. "Connie's car is parked under the tarp. Probably due for maintenance, but it should make getting around town easier."

Before Kari could answer, Angel appeared at the bottom of the stairs. "Hey, good I caught you. I'm having them move all the furniture and boxes into the dining room, for now, to get them out of the way, but we can put it wherever you want." He gestured for her to follow him to the living room, where a floor jack had been set up in the corner, and most of the drywall covering the ceiling had been pulled off, leaving it bare.

"Coming through, watch out below," a yell came from above.

Angel reached out and ushered Kari away from the living room door. The brief bump of his arm made her all too aware of her attraction to him. His expression remained pleasant and she assumed her feelings were probably one-sided.

She heard men moving upstairs. Their steps were cautious.

"This looks bad." Kari sighed. "I guess this means I should hold off on finding a real estate agent."

"Good news, we can fix it. The house is well built. Structurally sound. There was just too much weight concentrated in the middle of that room for too long. Some of the boxes had bricks in them. And jars of what looked like brick dust. That combined with old water damage, and you get..." He pointed at the hole.

"What the hell, Connie," Kari muttered. Then to Angel, she said, "Bricks, really?"

He nodded.

"I don't know what that's about." Kari rubbed her eyes and shook her head. "Are they *valuable* bricks?"

"They're old. Look neat. You might be able to sell them. Reclaimed items can bring some money in the right markets. I can ask around if you want."

Kari shook her head and walked onto the front porch. "I'll figure it out later. Maybe put the bricks out back for now? No reason to keep them in the dining room. Or the house."

"Can do." Angel nodded. He walked with her as she went around the side of the house where a tarp covered Connie's car.

"Is there anything else?" Kari bounced the keys in her palm.

His eyes lingered on her hand before moving

briefly to her chest. He quickly averted his eyes. "Yeah, actually, a few of the guys saw your cinnamon rolls out on the table and thought they were fair game. They ate through the pan before I had a chance to stop them. If you tell me where you got them, I'll replace them."

Kari laughed. "Don't worry about it. Tell you what, help me get this tarp off, and we'll call it even."

He reached to help her pull it from the car. "What do you have under there?"

"Not sure." When they managed to get it off the vehicle, she frowned. "A nineties era sedan that has seen too much sun if the oxidized paint chips are to be believed. I have it on good authority that it needs maintenance."

For someone who always bragged about being rich, Connie hadn't been acting like it. The only reason Connie would have a car like this would have been to hide her identity. Or she squandered the family fortune and Kari was about to inherit a stack of bills.

"Not quite like the movies when they find a nineteen fifty-one Merc under the tarp in perfect condition and go on a wild adventure," Kari added.

"I'm not sure I've watched those movies. I tend to like shows with explosions and spies." Angel began folding the tarp. "Nineteen fifty-one Merc is fairly specific. You like old cars?"

"Not particularly. I covered the classic car circuit for an auto magazine for a few months. I wasn't the best person for the job, but I was the only person within range to get there in time. Car photography isn't my specialty." Kari unlocked the trunk so that he could drop the tarp inside.

Seeing a box of old mason jars, Angel grabbed them. "I'll put these behind the house for you, so they don't clank around."

When he started to walk away, she called after him, "Hey, wait, can I ask...?"

"You don't have to ask me if you can ask me." He grinned.

"So I've been told," she said more to herself. "Heather Warwick, is she, you know, all there?"

"Warrick," he corrected. His body language changed, and he stiffened a little in defense. "She's solid. That whole family is good people. William and Heather will give you their last dollar if they think you need it."

"I didn't mean to offend," she tried to backtrack. "She seems nice."

"I think she's sad after losing her son," he said. "Maybe that's why you ask if something is off about her. Funerals can't be easy. I imagine it made her relive old memories. Parents never get over pain like that."

"I didn't know." Kari felt horrible. "Thank you for telling me. I'll be more sensitive when I talk to her."

Angel nodded. "I'm going to put these out back and then get to it."

She watched him walk around the corner of the house and disappear from sight.

"Good job, Kari," she grumbled as she got into the musty car. The engine started a little rough, but at least it started. "Way to offend the people helping you out."

CHAPTER FIVE

THE SMELL of coffee and the low murmur of conversations filled the local coffee shop. They blended together in the music of white noise accompanied by the grunting of the bean grinder and the hiss of foam. The logo matched the cup Heather had brought her that morning and only made Kari feel guilty again for what she'd asked Angel. The woman had lost a son. So what if Heather wanted to believe the ghosts of loved ones still lingered?

Kari had found a small table in the corner, tucked away from the rest of the customers. People flowed through the line from the door, looping around to the counter. Displays showcased everything from hand-made jewelry to paintings to tea tins to t-shirts. The owner had opened one wall in the narrow room to connect to a bookstore next door.

"Janey, you're up!" the guy behind the counter yelled as he set down the customer's coffee cup.

Kari turned her attention to the large manila envelope given to her at the law offices of Johansen, Elliot, and Snyder. As the only living relative, Connie's will had been simple and straightforward. Kari received pretty much everything, and the lawyer was only too happy to speed through the appointment by handing her the packet without going through the details. He'd mentioned something about being late for a golf game.

Kari sighed. "Pretty much everything" included properties she knew nothing about: land in Louisiana, stock shares in a food company and a tobacco company, a couple of commercial properties, residential properties, several warehouses, something with chickens, about two million dollars in miscellaneous assets, and a Mississippi furniture store. Then there was the Freewild Cove house and paint-peeled sedan.

Seeing a smaller sealed envelope in the stack, Kari pulled it out. Her name was printed on the outside in Connie's handwriting. It was dated six years prior. She drew the edge of her finger along the seam to tear it open. Her hands shook. She wondered what Connie felt needed saying after her death, rather than while they were together.

Kari, she read. *You would not have been my first choice in heirs, but you are the only living relative, so taking care of the family properties falls on you. They tell me it's not legally advisable to demand you have a baby of proper breeding before you get your inheritance, which I think is bullshit, but for the love of your family, we cannot let the bloodline die with you. Because I worry that you will never get your act together, I had some eggs cryogenically frozen and have interviewed surrogates...*

Kari dropped the letter, not finishing it, and whispered, "What the hell, Connie?"

Connie would have been in her late seventies when she wrote the letter. What was she talking about, harvesting eggs at that age? Kari was no IVF specialist, but she doubted Connie would have been a good candidate for it. Even if Connie had done it in her thirties or forties, would those little popsicle aunts and uncles still be usable? Did Connie expect her to hire the human incubators to create more family members?

"Are you okay?"

Kari looked up in surprise as someone lightly touched her shoulder.

"You're crying," the woman noted. Curly red hair

framed her concerned expression, and she used her body to block the view of most of the shop in an attempt to give Kari privacy.

Kari automatically touched her face, finding tears. "Oh, I..."

"I don't mean to intrude. I'm Sue Jewel. I own the bookstore next door. If you'd like to come over, it's a little more private." Sue glanced around, and Kari realized people were staring at her.

Kari nodded and scooped up her papers. Sue took the coffee from the table and carried it for her. "Through here."

Sue led the way under the arch between the two stores. A white cat rested on a bookshelf as if standing guard over the coffee shop entrance.

"That's Ace," Sue said. "He's my business partner. This is his home base, but he pretty much reigns over every business on this block."

"Nice to meet you, Ace," Kari said, shifting the papers in her arms, so she could pet the cat as she passed.

"Meh," the cat said, rolling on his side. He knocked a book off the shelf.

"Did he just say meh?" Kari asked in surprise.

"That's his meow. He's a special kitty. Come with me. There is a couch in the back," Sue offered, returning to pick up the book off the floor. She placed it away from where Ace rested.

"I like your shop," Kari said.

Ace walked along the top of the shelf and batted the book back onto the floor.

"Thanks. I haven't owned it long." If Sue heard the book fall a second time, she didn't show it.

Sue walked through the book aisles and around a hollow square-shaped sales counter in the middle of the shop. Tall bookshelves were to the left of the counter with handwritten signs to denote sections.

"Do you own the coffee shop, too?"

"That would be Jameson Lloyd." Sue glanced over her shoulder and grinned. "We've been dating for about two years now. It's all very romance movie of the week. Coffee shop guy hooking up with the bookstore gal."

Ace zipped past Kari's feet and ran to the right of the counter, to where a low platform stage had been set up with rows of folding chairs around it. A couch sat against a wall, hidden from view of the coffee shop. The cat leaped onto a blanket arranged on the back of a couch in what appeared to be his well-worn spot. "Meow."

Sue put the coffee down on a small table next to the couch.

"You are welcome to stay as long as you like." Sue touched a silver ring on her finger and began agitating it.

"Thank—" Kari's hand tingled, and she looked at the ring she'd found in the storage room. Her gaze briefly traced the patterns. She put the papers on the couch. Whispering, she managed, "Thank you."

"Vivien mentioned there was someone else who'd found a ring," Sue said. "I admit, it still kind of freaks me out when the awareness happens."

Kari tried to pull the band off, but it wouldn't budge. Freewild Cove was apparently some kind of new-age-y colony. Strange that Connie would call such a place home.

"I'm really not the one to explain it." Sue shifted uncomfortably. "At least not with this."

"Why is everyone going on about rings?" Kari tugged harder, but the jewelry only turned on her finger. It didn't feel like it was too tight.

"They belonged to Julia Warrick. The women who find them are meant to have them." Sue sat on the couch. "Has weird stuff been happening to you lately? Does it seem like the television is giving you messages? Are things moving around on their own?"

Kari glanced over her shoulder. Voices came from the coffee shop, but the bookstore was empty. What nutcase rabbit hole of a town did Connie move to? No, the television wasn't talking directly to her. She didn't see ghosts and objects were not moving on their own.

But the projector had been playing in a locked room and did catch on fire. That was strange.

"Maybe if I tell you what happened to me, you'll feel better discussing whatever you're going through. After my husband died…" Sue closed her eyes briefly. "After he tried killing me and ended up killing himself instead, I started seeing strange things in my house. The television turned on when it wasn't plugged in. The channels flipped erratically, only pausing long enough to use the words it needed to give me a message. The remote floated in the air. Signs pointed me to Freewild Cove. Does any of this sound…?" She gave a small laugh and stood from the couch. "I can see by your expression the answer is no. Ignore me, then. I sound insane."

"I, uh…" Kari wanted to stop Sue from leaving. She didn't want to be alone. Taking a deep breath, she said, "There was an old home movie projector playing in a locked room."

Sue returned to the couch and patted the seat next to her. Ace rested near her neck. "Tell me about it."

"That's it." Kari sat next to the woman. "My grand-mother had a locked storage room, and after her funeral, I heard a noise behind the door. There was a light coming from underneath. When I broke inside, a home movie was playing of my mother when she was young. I'd never seen it before. I didn't even know we had old family movies."

"Did your mother say anything? Was she doing anything in it?"

"It was one of those old, silent eight-millimeter films." Kari held up her ring finger. "My mother's image pointed, and when I followed the direction of her finger, I found this ring."

Sue sighed and nodded. "Yep, that sounds like a Julia clue."

"I mean, there's a logical explanation. The projector could have been on some kind of timer." Kari wasn't sure who she was trying to convince. "I might have had a few drinks."

"Did you see a timer?"

"I didn't have a chance to look because the film caught fire. Then I tripped into a wall of boxes filled with bricks. They crashed through the second-story floor, and I fell through the living room ceiling." Kari lifted the coffee cup and wrapped her fingers around it for warmth.

"Yeah, I heard about the floor thing." Sue reached behind her head to pet Ace.

"You heard?"

"Small town." Sue chuckled. "Gossip moves faster than 5G technology, and it all passes through the coffee shop. As much as I hate it, everyone found out about my ex trying to kill me. A detective talked to the local police, and there you go, 5G gossip."

"Your husband really tried to kill you?" Kari had no reason to doubt what Sue said, but it seemed unreal.

"Yep." Sue sighed, turning her attention toward petting Ace. "He was on his way to bury me when he wrecked our car and died. I was thrown from the trunk."

"I don't know what to say," Kari admitted. "That sucks major ass."

Sue snorted a tiny laugh and turned her attention back to Kari. "He was a major asshole."

"So, all that weird stuff you said was happening? You think it was your ex haunting you?"

If asked point-blank, Kari would say she didn't believe in ghosts. Scary stories were fun around a campfire when strangers became friends on the transient road. Yet, something about the way Sue spoke made her want to believe her. The woman gave an impression of genuine honesty mixed with slight embarrassment.

"I think Hank had so much anger in life that it just

simmered into his afterlife. Transferred energy from one state of being to another. All that rage had to go somewhere, and it manifested itself the same way it had when he was alive. It came after me." Sue rubbed the bridge of her nose as if to keep her eyes from tearing. "I know it's been two years, but in many ways, it's still a little fresh. I still get jumpy when I'm alone at night."

"I'd imagine it's hard to get over a betrayal like that," Kari said.

"It's better now. I have Jameson, this business, great friends. It makes all the bad in my life...well, not exactly worth it, but it gives it an ending and allows me to have a happier chapter." Sue waved her hands in dismissal as she stood. "Forgive the book metaphors. When all you think about is reading and books, you tend to get stuck in that world."

"I get your meaning," Kari said.

"It looks like you have work to do. I'll leave you to it, but if you want to talk, I'm here."

When Sue left her alone, Kari eyed the cat. "So, ghosts, eh?"

"Meh," Ace answered, turning his attention toward licking his paw.

"Right." Kari looked at the stack of papers from the lawyer and picked up her grandmother's letter. Then, grabbing the coffee, she closed her eyes as she tilted her head back to take a drink. The motion gave her a small head rush.

Kari opened her eyes to find she was looking at the textured popcorn ceiling of Connie's guest room. She jumped to her feet. "What the hell?"

The coffee slipped from her hand, spilling down her shirt and crashing to the floor. Kari clutched the letter, but the lawyer's file was missing. She felt the hot liquid adhering the material to her stomach.

"Why does this keep happening?" She took a deep breath and tried to steady her nerves.

This time, Kari hadn't been drinking, so liquor couldn't be to blame. It didn't feel like she was blacking out and losing time, especially since the coffee was hot and the letter was still in her fist.

"Come on, guys, let's get as much as we can done before the owner gets back." The loud clap of his hands followed Angel's shout. "She's a nice lady who has enough on her plate. She doesn't need us banging around."

The sound of construction instantly flooded the house.

Kari dropped the letter on the bed, then tugged off the suit jacket and tossed it aside. She sat down, not caring that coffee had created a puddle on the floor or that her cooling shirt clung to her chest. Her body ached and the stitches on her leg itched.

Seeing the flask on the nightstand, she grabbed it. There wasn't much left inside but the burn of liquor was welcome, though not more so than the idea of oblivion. When the flask was empty, she reached under the bed for the full bottle to take a few more gulps. She fell back onto the mattress to stare at the ceiling.

Connie might have been a piece of work, but she'd been family.

Maybe she was being punished.

I didn't do anything.

The loud banging only made Kari feel isolated and alone, trapped under the fake silver stars of the ugly guest-room ceiling. She tried to imagine she was lying under the desert's night sky, but the sound kept drawing her back to reality. A man shouted for more nails, and someone turned on classic rock.

Kari didn't want to talk to anyone. She didn't want to think.

Fatigue made it impossible to contemplate what she should do next. Her heavy eyelids dropped even as she tried to keep them open.

"I don't want to deal with any of this," she whispered.

CHAPTER SIX

KARI OPENED her eyes to find shadows creeping over the ceiling. A soft light came through the window. Sleep had not lifted the heavy weight pressing in on her chest. In fact, if anything, she felt worse. A mind-dulling fog had settled in her head, and the stitches on her leg throbbed.

As she pushed up, her hand crumpled Connie's letter. She'd fallen asleep next to it.

Kari lifted the note, seeing the words in the dim light, *Kari, You would not have been my first choice in heirs...*

She dropped her hand and put the letter back on the bed. No part of her wanted to continue reading the strange ramblings about frozen eggs and timeless guilt.

She'd had enough reminders of Connie's disappointments to last a thousand lifetimes.

Though dry, her shirt was stiff from the spilled coffee. She jerked it over her head in irritation and dropped it on the floor, only to replace it with a worn red t-shirt. Deep wrinkles were embedded in the loose slacks, and she still wore her shoes from earlier.

"Not winning any fashion shows," she grumbled to her reflection. "Fuck it all anyway."

Kari rubbed her face, trying to erase the black mascara smudges under her eyes.

The construction noise from before her nap had lessened to the occasional thud, and when she opened the bedroom door, it stopped altogether. Silence permeated the house. The air didn't stir, as if the oxygen had been sucked from the hallway, creating a vacuum. She found it difficult to breathe.

"Hello?" she called on her way to the stairs. "Angel, are you still here?"

She expected an answer since she'd just heard them working but received silence.

"Anyone?"

An eerie feeling came over her, vibrating up her hand from the ring.

Fwap-fwap-fwap...

Kari stumbled and caught herself against the wall.

For a moment, she couldn't move as chills worked their way over her.

...fwap-fwap-fwap-fwap-fwap...

"I hate this freaking house," she whispered. The first time she'd investigated the noise, she'd been half-convinced Connie had someone locked in the room. Now, knowing some sort of supernatural fire phenomenon waited to throw her through the floor, she didn't want to investigate. Because what else could all of this be but paranormal? Hauntings might not exist, but it would seem someone didn't tell the ghosts that.

Kari slowly turned toward the storage room. Light came from behind the cracked door. She stared at it dancing over the broken frame from when she'd busted it open.

...fwap-fwap-fwap...

She thought about running down the stairs and out the front door. If she got in her RV, she could drive away. She could disappear. There was nothing for her in Freewild Cove.

Would she be transported back? What if she was driving and suddenly disappeared? If her RV wrecked and hurt someone, she would never be able to forgive herself.

It was the only thing that could have made her face her fear and turn toward the storage room.

"Is someone in there?" She tried to project her voice but failed.

Kari thought of the projection of her mother. The desire to connect with her past drew her to the door. Her feet slid, one shaky step, two...three...

"Mom?" she whispered. "Connie? Is that you?"

Had Connie's ghost manipulated the projector? Is that how it started in a locked room?

Kari lightly bumped the door with the back of her hand, forcing it open. The noise stopped.

She reached for the light switch and breathed a sigh of relief when it came on. There was no projector. Angel and his crew had fixed the floor, at least temporarily. Plywood covered where the hole had been. Angel and his workers had moved the clutter to leave the room mostly empty.

"It's just a room in an old house," she said, trying to comfort herself and prove she was brave at the same time. "The fire was a freak accident, and all this talk of ghosts is messing with my sanity."

Kari stepped cautiously toward the repaired floor, pressing her toe to listen to the creaking wood. The overhead light flickered and went dark.

Fwap-fwap-fwap...

Light from a different source flashed. She spun toward it, unable to keep the scream from erupting from her lungs. The flickering image of her mother stood in the middle of the room, no projector, no screen on which to host her 2D body, no background from the past to contain her.

...fwap-fwap-fwap...

"M-mom?" Kari could barely push the sound past her lips.

The *fwap* of the ghost projector continued as her mother's 2D image turned fully toward her and pointed at the floor where Kari had found the ring. The direction of her finger had changed, but the area she pointed toward remained the same. Before, she had gestured to the side, and now she pointed forward. Her mother's gaze focused on her as she moved as if following Kari as she tried to stumble her way toward the door.

Multiple footsteps thundered up the stairs. The noise echoed the rapid beats of Kari's heart drumming their way into her ears.

"Kari, where are you? Are you all right?" Lorna called. "What happened?"

"Kari?" Vivien yelled.

"Kari—" Heather began as the sound of her voice reached the doorway. "She's in here."

Kari didn't move as she heard them enter behind her.

"Oh, fuck, that's creepy. My haunting didn't do that," Sue whispered. "Is this normal?

No one answered her, at least not that Kari could make out.

"Kari?" Heather asked, touching her shoulder.

The human contact startled her, and she jerked away. Sue, Lorna, Vivien, and Heather stood in the room with her, inadvertently blocking the door. She turned her attention back to her mother.

"Do you know who that is?" Heather asked. "She seems to be watching you."

"My mom, Lori." Kari nodded, unable to take her eyes off the ghostly image. Her mother's lips moved, but the filmed image was silent beyond the rhythmic *fwap-fwap-fwap.*

"What's she pointing at?" Sue asked.

"The floor," Vivien answered, a little too dryly.

"Because Kari fell through it?" Sue insisted.

"Shh," someone shushed the questions.

"Ask her," Heather prodded, giving Kari a light tap on her arm. "It doesn't look like she wants to hurt you."

...fwap-fwap-fwap...

"Mom? What are you pointing at?" Kari whispered. She tried to inch closer to the image, but her legs shook too severely, and she felt any movement would unlock her knees and send her to the floor.

"Keep talking to her," Heather encouraged.

Kari turned her head toward the woman but kept her eyes focused on meeting her mother's gaze. "What do I say?"

"Just engage her," Heather urged. "Try to focus her attention on the moment and find out what she wants."

"Mom," Kari said louder though the words were breathless. "It's me. Kari. Your daughter. We didn't get a chance to meet when I was born, did we? But I know you. I've seen pictures anyway, so I know who you are. I... Connie, um, your mom raised me. She raised you too, so that kind of connects us. Was she miserable when you were little? Maybe she missed you? Maybe she was just that way inclined, you know, being ill-tempered. I, uh, I..."

"You're doing good," Heather said. "She's still here. Keep talking."

...*fwap-fwap-fwap*...

"I don't know if you know this, but Connie passed away." Kari could barely choke out the words past the guilt she felt. She remembered the feel of the pillow in her hands.

...*fwap-fwap-fwap*...

"I used to daydream that you were alive and would come to find me with my father," Kari continued. "Every Christmas morning, I would run down. I was convinced if I was really good all year, that would be the best present Santa could bring me."

Lori lifted her hand and drew it down insistently to point toward the floor again.

"I found the ring." Kari showed the jewelry on her finger. "See."

Her mother's arm began to twitch violently as if trying to draw her attention back to the floor.

"Maybe we should stop. I think we're making it mad," Sue said.

"Her," Lorna corrected.

"Yeah," Sue amended, "making her mad."

"Viv, can you sense anything?" Lorna asked. "Heather?"

...fwap-fwap-fwap...

"I've never seen a ghost manifest like this," Heather said. "Kari, keep talking to her. Maybe you can get her to interact more. Make your words personal. Connect to shared emotion."

"Mom," Kari took a deep breath. "Connie refused to talk about you. I've seen pictures. I know you took ballet when you were little. So did I. And once in middle school, I found one of your old books in a storage box. You'd written your name in it. After that, I started writing my L's like you."

...fwap-fwap-fwap...

"Mom, there is so much I want to ask you." Kari took a deep breath. "Who's my father? I know he's dead. I tried to look up bus accidents the day I was born, but—"

...fwa—

"—*ah!*" Kari screamed as flames lit up her mother's image. She jumped back from the intense heat, knocking into someone as she lifted her arms to block the sudden burst.

Lori disappeared into glowing embers that dissipated before touching the floor. The overhead light flickered several times before turning back on.

"Mom?" Kari trembled. Hands gripped her arms, steadying her from behind. She wanted to break free but was too weak. Hot tears trailed down her cheeks. "Where did she go?"

Kari looked at the women fully for the first time since they'd entered the room. Lorna let go of her arms and gave her an understanding smile. Sue held the manila envelope from the law office that Kari had left in the bookstore when she'd been transported back to the house. Vivien had moved closer to the patched hole and knelt as she searched the empty floor where Lori had indicated. Kari didn't know what the woman hoped to find.

Heather lifted her hands and slowly stepped

forward, sweeping them through the air to feel for Lori. "I can't detect anything. I think she's gone for now."

Kari wondered what the fire meant. Was her mother trapped in actual Hell?

"What else was with the ring when you found it?" Vivien asked.

As the shock of seeing the ghostly image began to wear off, Kari became grateful she wasn't alone. "Nothing. Someone had made a nook out of boxes filled with bricks, and there was a projector aimed at an old sheet. I guess Connie could have done it, but she wasn't in the best of health since moving back here. I don't see her hauling bricks. The ring was wedged between two boxes. The second I touched it, the fire started, and I..." Kari gestured at the floor.

"Aren't bricks used in some spells?" Sue asked. "I read something about it at the bookstore."

"Brick dust," Heather said. "For protection. I think it's mostly done in Louisiana, though. I've never heard of whole bricks meaning anything."

"Maybe they're enchanted bricks," Sue surmised.

"Angel said there were jars of brick dust too," Kari said.

"I used bricks to break Rex's car windows once." Vivien gave a wry chuckle. "I found them very useful.

Maybe Connie has unfinished business in the form of a vehicle hit list."

Kari thought, *Yeah, that sounds like Connie, all right.*

"Twice," Heather corrected. "You broke Rex's windows twice."

"No, the second time was with his favorite gulf club." Vivien shrugged. "He deserved it."

"Was this after you caught him cheating on you?" Lorna asked.

"No, I don't care about that. Those coked-out hookers did me a favor. They gave me the push I needed to cut the dead weight from my life," Vivien said. "What he did was much worse. I used the brick from a house that he'd helped foreclose on, which put a widower and his three kids out on the street. They bulldozed it before anyone could intervene. The golf club was because he'd been trying to find loopholes in the law to move a large percentage of charitable donations meant to feed people into the administrative paychecks of his golfing buddies. So now I use the video of him snorting drugs off a hooker's ass to keep his law firm from jacking with my alimony payments, which I then use to fund charities. I think karma would approve."

"I bet you anything she also bought that widower a house," Lorna whispered to Kari.

Vivien glanced at Lorna but didn't say one way or the other.

"You have video of your ex-husband with prostitutes?" Kari got the impression Vivien wasn't joking. "Wait, you said his name was Rex? That's the name of the lawyer I met with today for Connie's estate."

"You went to the law firm of Jerk Face, Expensive, and Spray Tan—I mean, Johansen, Elliot, and Snyder?" Vivien gave a tiny shiver of disgust.

Kari nodded. One of the guys in the lobby photos did have a distinctively unnatural tan.

"Yep, that would be my ex's firm." Vivien shook her head. "Don't worry. Rex is good at his job. I'm sure the estate is in order. If it's not, I'll take you with me when I slash the tires on his new sports car. It's very therapeutic."

"Viv, stop. She's not going to know you're joking and is going to think you're a vandal." Heather examined the patched floor and pressed on it with her foot.

"Sometimes, you need to get the point across," Vivien continued. "Rex loves his cars more than people, and he cares too much about his reputation to have me arrested for it. I married the jerk and helped his career. I ignored my gut feelings and made excuses for his lack of empathy. I feel morally responsible to keep him cosmically in line."

"So, uh..." Kari took a deep breath, trying to get the topic back to her mother. The normal conversation about exes and lawyers somehow didn't fit the supernatural strangeness of their current situation, and the fact that the others seemed unaffected by it all indicated this had happened to them more than once.

Kari watched Heather's feet as she walked over the patch.

"Angel does great work," Heather said, more to herself.

Lorna gently touched her shoulder. "How are you doing with all this? I know it's a lot to take in."

"I think I'm ready to admit weird things have been happening to me." Kari tried to smile but failed.

"Ya think?" Vivien chuckled.

"Welcome to the magic club," Lorna said.

"Can't we get the book and call the spirit back?" Sue asked. "Or maybe ask Julia?"

"Book? What book?" Kari glanced at each of them for answers. She wanted her mother to come back. In many ways, she still felt like that little girl reaching out into nothingness, wishing that the woman would come and take her from Connie.

"Julia left us a séance book that helps us contact

the dead." Heather pressed her hands against her temples and suppressed a yawn. "Lorna, please tell me you brought something sugary. I feel like the energy has been sucked from the room."

"The air does feel heavy in here," Sue agreed.

"Lemon cupcakes," Lorna answered.

"That's right. You said Julia was friends with Connie." Kari stopped Heather from leaving, not ready to go. "Didn't you also say she was...?"

"Dead," Vivien supplied. "Yep."

"And you still..." Kari looked at where her mother had been and knew she had her answer. "Got it."

"Like I said, welcome to the magic club." Lorna walked out the door. "Come on. Sugar now means we'll feel better later. It helps counteract the energy drain spirits can cause."

"Mm, yes, please." Vivien hurried to follow her.

Sue paused awkwardly in the doorway, appearing more troubled than the others. She clearly wanted to say something but held back. Glancing at the envelope in her hand, she quickly stepped forward to hand it to Kari before leaving.

"You said there were boxes?" Heather lightly touched Kari's arm, urging her to follow Sue out of the storage room.

"Angel had them moved to the backyard." Kari didn't want to leave. What if Lori came back and she wasn't there to see it? "He said they were all filled with bricks. It was too much weight on the floor. When I knocked them over, the weight is what caused me to fall into the living room."

"Maybe this is like a needle in a haystack," Heather said. "Who would think to dig through boxes of bricks?"

Vivien suddenly appeared back in the doorway. "Whoa, whoa, whoa, hold on a minute."

"What?" Kari spun back around, hoping to see her mother.

"Someone is attracted to Angel," Vivien stated. "I'm picking up some serious psychic energy like I could feel your insides blushing from the hallway."

"What?" Kari shook her head in denial. "No. I don't have time to think about... No."

"Who doesn't have time to think about getting a little action?" Vivien laughed. "Isn't that the whole reason we pair up?"

"Nice," Heather drawled wryly. "I'm going to mention that to Troy next time I see him."

"Fine, you got me. I'm in *looove*." Vivien playfully rolled her eyes. "We get together for all the emotional connection love stuff too. But I'm not ashamed to say I like having fun. Sex is fun. And there're proven health benefits to it too."

"I can't. There's just so much..." Kari shook her head. Yes, she was attracted to Angel. He was an attractive man—rough working hands, friendly smile, kind heart... "No."

"Your mouth says no, but the energy you're throwing off says *yes*." Vivien winked.

"Easy, matchmaker." Heather tried to shoo Vivien from the room. "One thing at a time."

"You want me to get a read on him and tell you if he's into you?" Vivien asked.

"What? Are you going to pass him a note after class for me like in middle school?" Kari blurted before she could stop herself.

Vivien laughed. "If you like. Or I could use my magical gifts. They're much more efficient."

Before Kari could ask what the woman meant by that, Vivien left the haunted storage room.

"I feel like I have fifty billion questions in my head," Kari said. "And none of them are coming into focus."

"It's the energy your mother needed to manifest. Spirits can't come from thin air. When there aren't enough lights or electricity, they take from people. In séances, we take precautions. But when they just appear, it can be more difficult to control. It can leave you feeling tired and unable to focus. It's why Lorna always travels with sugary baked goods for us."

"Sugar sounds good," Kari said.

Heather took her arm. "Your mother wanted us to search for something. Let's go outside and check the bricks to find out what she's trying to say."

CHAPTER SEVEN

"Lorna, are you sure your finder magic can't tell us if anything is hidden in here?" Vivien asked.

"I tried," Lorna answered, not for the first time. "If there is anything in these boxes, I don't think it's meant for me to find."

Kari alternated between biting the lemon cupcake with one hand and removing bricks from a box with the other as she knelt on the grass in the backyard. Angel had stacked Connie's brick collection in a cluster, four boxes high and an endless-row long against the back wall of the house.

Vivien and Heather worked next to her. The motion sensor light hadn't turned on and evening darkened the landscape. Lorna and Sue held their phones to shine light with their flashlight apps while they worked.

Sue shone her light over the stacks of boxes. "There has to be an easier way to search through these. If we make sure no one is looking, maybe I can make a mess and then clean it up." Sue waved her hand toward the boxes. "Or maybe not."

Kari wasn't sure what the woman meant.

"I think there's some kind of protection or repellant magic on them," Heather said.

"Just once, I wish spirits would come right out and say what they wanted," Lorna stated. Her light wavered as she looked around.

"Yeah, I can hear it now," Vivien chuckled before lowering her voice. "Good evening, ladies. I am a demon. I have come to haunt you, scare you, and ultimately drag your soul to eternal damnation while I take over your body and wear you like a skin suit. So very nice to meet you."

"They're rarely straightforward." Heather frowned and swatted at her ear. "And often annoying."

"I noticed you were distracted. Which one is it tonight?" Vivien asked.

Heather closed her eyes and took a deep, steadying breath.

"Oh, no. Muffy?" Lorna made a face. "She's back? Already?"

"Yep," Heather said under her breath while focusing on digging through the box. She carefully set bricks on the ground in a pile as if the task took a lot of her concentration.

Talking like a valley girl from the eighties, Vivien said, "Heather, like, I'm like totally sorry like that you have to like listen to like that grody like-likerton."

Kari looked around the yard but didn't see anyone. The others held very still, except for Heather, who kept working. "Who's Muffy?"

"A ghost," Lorna said.

Kari again glanced around. The cupcake and brick slid from her hands. She stood and backed toward Sue and Lorna. "Where? I don't see it."

"You won't," Sue answered. "Not unless they manifest or we séance them."

"They're all around," Lorna said. "Heather sees them."

"It's her magical power," Sue explained.

"It's her gift," Lorna amended. "She's a born medium like her grandmother Julia. They don't need séances to communicate with the dead. Their entire life is a giant séance."

Heather pressed her hands against her head. "I

wouldn't exactly call it a gift right now. Usually, I can block the noise if I concentrate hard enough, but this..." She let loose a long sigh. "It's gotten worse since I first found Julia's ring in my tax box. Honestly, I thought taxes were headache-inducing enough on their own. Now I have ghosts yelling in my ear all the time. They keep getting louder and more persistent."

Kari lifted her arm and gave a quick sweep through the air. "How can you tell when they're around?"

"We can't," Lorna said. "Unless they manifest like Sue said."

"I still have a hard time taking a shower." Sue wrinkled her nose. "I'm paranoid they're in there watching me."

"They probably are," Vivien laughed. "Perverts die too. The afterlife is a long time. You should give them a show. Let them see what they're missing."

Heather moaned softly and pressed a finger to her temple.

Kari shivered, thinking of all the private moments she wouldn't want a ghost watching. "That's a terrifying thought."

"You know, I've always meant to ask. Do ghosts masturbate or have sex?" Sue asked. "Or do those drives go away like eating and breathing?"

Lorna gave a half-laugh, half-choke of surprise, and began coughing as she lightly patted her chest.

"I'm serious," Sue insisted. "Heather said that sometimes ghosts are locked in their death moment, so if someone died having sex then—?"

"Just shut up," Heather demanded, covering her ears.

"I'm sorry." Sue dropped her hand and the light with it.

Heather tucked her chin against her chest and groaned louder.

"Muffy, stop giving Heather migraines," Vivien ordered. "Just because you got drunk and fell off a boat doesn't mean you have to torture her with your incessant whining about it. She gets it. Being dead sucks. Go get a hobby, like watching people in changing rooms or haunting the food court at the mall. Whatever it is you eighties kids like to do."

Kari watched in silence, not sure what to make of the interaction.

"Please stop shouting." Heather moaned louder. "Fine, fine, I'll tell her. Viv, Muffy didn't get drunk and fall off the boat. She tripped, and her coward husband failed to dive into the ocean and save her."

"It's been like forty years," Vivien directed over Heather's shoulder. "Time to move on, sweetheart."

"No, I'm not repeating..." Heather frowned in annoyance.

"What is she saying? Is Muffy miffed?" Vivien mocked.

"Muffy, please stop screaming," Heather begged. "I'm not saying that."

"Tell me what she's saying," Vivien said. "I can take anything she tries to dish out."

Kari tilted her head, trying to listen for whatever Heather heard. Had this been any other night, she would have assumed this was a performance. After seeing her mother's image projected from nothingness, she knew it wasn't a joke.

Kari took another step back, away from Heather and the supernatural interaction. A chill worked over her. She stared into the shadows, trying to see any subtle shift in the light that would indicate a ghost stood amongst them.

"She said you're one to talk since it took you like thirty years to get over your dead beach bum husband." Heather pressed her palms to her ears. "And she is calling you a few choice names."

"Muffy, so help me, I'm going to exorcise your annoying ass and send you straight to—" Vivien gasped as her hair blew away from her face. Her arms flung in the air as an invisible force propelled her backward.

The sound of her heels dragging across the lawn ended when she landed on her back with a loud thud. "*Oomph.*"

"Vivien!" Lorna dropped her phone and ran to where Vivien had fallen on the ground. "Don't move. Are you hurt?"

"I'm fine. My ass broke my fall." Vivien swatted at Lorna's hands when the woman tried to check her. "Did it work? Did I piss her off enough to leave?"

Heather dropped her hands and sighed in relief. "Yeah, she's gone. Thank you."

"Good." Vivien frowned and rubbed her hip.

"What just happened?" Kari whispered, afraid the ghost might be listening and would turn her supernatural attention to the rest of them.

"Muffy expended her energy pushing Vivien over. It'll be a while before she builds up enough to manifest again," Lorna answered, then to Vivien, she added, "I hate when you do that. Someday you're going to really be hurt."

"That's why I have you, my magical medic," Vivien teased. She slowly pushed up from the ground. "Oh crap, Muffy was pissed. I need to cuddle a basket of kittens or something. I can feel her anger and annoyance pressing in on me like an emotional straitjacket."

"Are there others here?" Kari asked.

Heather glanced around. Her eyes lingered on the distance a little too long. "No."

Kari followed her gaze, not believing her.

"We can finish this in the morning." Kari looked at the back of the house and then turned to see her RV parked nearby. The urge to leave was strong, but she knew she couldn't go for all the reasons she'd already considered. Besides, could she live with herself if she didn't learn everything she could about her mother?

"Hey." Vivien gently touched her arm. "I know that running away feels like it will be easier because that's what you've done in the past, but you can't run from fate. Everyone needs human contact, friends. Let us be yours. You've been alone on the road for too long."

"I have friends." Kari stared at the RV.

"No. You have friendly acquaintances. That's not the same thing." Vivien turned Kari to meet her gaze. "Bricks run in the family, don't they?"

"You mean because I inherited...?" Kari wished everyone would just say what they meant. Every time they tried to tell her something, it became another fucking riddle to solve.

"Okay. You want blunt. Connie had hers in that room, guarding whatever secrets we are going to find. But you built bricks around yourself, like the lady in a tower, to keep you safe from the world. No one can scale that high wall and get too close. You watch everyone from a distance and hide if they even try to reach you. Who can blame you? From what I sense about Connie, I think it's a miracle you're not completely emotionally screwed up."

"She doesn't mean anything by that," Lorna put forth quickly. "We're all screwed up. I mean, I was married to a man who had a first wife that he never divorced that I knew nothing about for decades. When he died, and I tried to summon him back for closure, we let loose a demon that tried to kill me."

"I already told you about my husband, who died trying to kill me and then came back from the dead to finish the job," Sue said. "He beat me for years, and I stayed with him because I was too scared to leave. I know what it's like to feel alone."

Kari looked at Vivien.

"You heard what Muffy said about me." Vivien sighed. "For decades, I carried a torch for my first husband, who died of cancer shortly after we were married right out of high school. I wouldn't let anyone break through to my heart until I met Troy."

"And you?" Kari asked Heather. The second she said it, she wished she could take the question back. Angel had mentioned Heather's son.

"Her heart broke in another way," Lorna said, shifting her weight to shield Heather from view as if automatically trying to protect her.

"I lost my son when he was very young. After that, the world became...less..." Heather let her words drift away as she didn't finish the thought. No doubt some things were too painful to talk about.

"I'm sorry." Kari's hand tingled from the ring. The sensation was distracting and seemed to radiate all the way to her scalp. She ran her fingers through her hair, trying to get the lightheaded feeling to stop. "Yes, the nomadic life is lonely, but no one tried to kill me. I wasn't married. I have no children. All I had was Connie and being raised by an emotionally distant woman is hardly the same thing you all went through."

"And yet you're here with one of Julia's rings, which means you've come to us for a reason. You have some past hurts that need to be healed. Who are we to judge the depth of damage your parents' deaths caused? Or Connie?" Heather gestured at the stacks of bricks on the ground. "You're searching for answers and closure just as we were, and you're not alone."

Their perception caused a slight tremor to work through Kari. In many ways, she feared she was too old to change. This is who she was—an emotionally stunted nomad who drove away whenever things got too close for comfort. She really, *really* wanted to get in her RV and drive. There was a comfort to the endless roads, the highway's center line coming at her in predictable patterns as she journeyed forward.

"So you touch people and make them feel better," Kari said to Lorna before pointing at Heather. "And you see ghosts." She gestured to Vivien. "You pick up on people's emotions and thoughts." Finally, she turned to Sue. "And you...?"

"I fix stuff," Sue said, "and clean."

"She's amazing with a jigsaw puzzle," Vivien added.

"You..." Kari frowned. "Clean? So no magic?"

"Uh." Sue glanced around to ensure the yard was empty before quickly gesturing toward the side of the house. She pointed at a piece of loose siding. It righted itself with an audible thud.

Kari's mouth opened, but no sound came out.

"And, um..." Sue motioned toward litter that had blown into the nearby bushes. A plastic bag and empty cup hovered in the air before flying around the side of the house. Moments later, the sound of a trashcan lid clanged.

"Kari? You all right? You look like you might throw up." Lorna reached for her.

"I'm trying to decide whether I scream and run, or

ask her to do it again," Kari managed weakly. The buzzing in her hand became more insistent. "I'm kind of jealous. They could have used that gift when cleaning out Connie's hoard upstairs."

"I wanted to call Sue when I saw your ceiling. It was the last thing you should have been dealing with the day of the funeral," Heather said. "With the paramedics coming in and out, it wasn't a good idea to get a magical fix. Very few know about what we can do, and we prefer to keep it that way."

"I did do a fast reclean for you when I saw the guys had left," Sue said.

"She has the best power ever gifted to anyone," Vivien said. "We haven't housecleaned since Sue moved into town."

"I'm not going to lie. It's awesome. I hate cleaning, so it's perfect." Sue laughed. "Late at night, I use it to rearrange the books that customers put back on the shelves in the wrong order. I don't want to get caught, so I've been talking to Jameson about putting in some blinds in the front window that I can pull down for privacy."

"You could use those Victorian-looking privacy screens. Lightweight, pretty, easy to move." Vivien opened another box of bricks. "Not like these things."

"Victorian? Because it's old-fashioned and print books are old-fashioned?" Sue joked.

"I didn't say that." Vivien arched a brow. "I like print books because I like having man candy on a cover, so I can show it off and shock people with what I'm reading."

"You would do that." Lorna chuckled, reaching to pick her phone off the ground to shine the light at Vivien.

"You know how most kids would hide a comic inside a chemistry book to at least pretend to be studying?" Heather asked. "Viv liked to shock the teachers with the most graphic horror comic she could find."

"That's because Mr. Horton was afraid of clowns, and he couldn't bring himself to look in my direction long enough to stop me. I do feel a little bad about it now. He was a decent teacher." Vivien laughed. "Conversely, Mrs. Parsons confiscated my romance novel and gave me some boring moralistic lecture about how it wasn't true literature, but I caught her self-righteous, hypocritical ass reading it after school."

"It's a wonder you graduated at all." Heather shook her head as she continued to search the bricks. She coughed and waved her hand in front of her face, only to explain, "Brick dust."

"Face it, Heather." Vivien opened a new box. "Our

lives were pretty much fiction as far as everyone else was concerned. If they didn't believe we had special gifts that they simply couldn't understand, then why should I believe in their science? I still say my answer to the essay question on the final arguing the existence of ghosts should have gotten an A."

Kari's childhood had been very different. "Connie would have put me in front of a firing squad for embarrassing her if I tried anything like that. She grounded me for getting a B on a test once and only let me out of my room to study with the tutors she hired. Failure was not an option in the Grove family."

"The more I learn about her..." Heather shook her head. "She sounds like a piece of work."

"She was definitely strongminded when it came to the way she liked things to be done," Kari answered.

"I wonder what your gift is, Kari," Lorna mused.

"I don't think I have one. I keep blacking out and ending up back at the house. I'm not sure it's a gift. It doesn't feel like it's coming from me." Kari walked toward the boxes and reached to check one on top of a new stack. The ring on her hand vibrated but stopped when she touched the box. She drew her fingers away, and it started vibrating again.

"Like a homing pigeon." Sue lifted her light higher

for Kari. "Always flying home no matter where you drop it off."

"I don't think I'm flying." Kari touched the box second from the top. The vibration lessened, only to start again when she let it go. She touched the third one down. The vibrations became stronger. "This one."

"That box?" Heather and Vivien joined her by the stack.

"I can't explain it. I just feel..." Kari looked at her hand as she pulled it away and then touched the box again.

"Feelings. That's good enough for me." Vivien reached for the top box. "Help me lift this down."

Kari, Heather, and Vivien pushed the box from the top and guided its heavy fall. Then followed it with the next one. They pried open the third box and began grabbing bricks out of it.

"It got cold all of a sudden, didn't it?" Sue said, visibly shivering. "Anyone else feel that?"

"Do you see anything?" Lorna asked.

When Vivien pulled out a brick near the center, Kari saw a wooden box nestled in the middle. Pretty designs were engraved on the top.

The second she touched it, lightning struck, followed by a loud *crack*. She jumped back in fright.

"What the...?" Heather looked toward the sky. "It's not supposed to storm tonight."

As if answering her declaration, fat droplets of rain began pelting them from the heavens. Lightning struck another time, stretching its long, crooked fingers over the darkness. Thunder boomed seconds later.

"Crap, that's close." Lorna stuck her phone under her shirt to protect it from the rain, hiding the light. "We need to get inside."

The wind kicked up, shifting the rain to fall at an angle.

Kari grabbed the box and automatically ran toward her RV instead of the house. When she opened the door to the living area, the stairs did not lower. The electricity was off. There was nowhere to plug in on Connie's lawn, and she hadn't wanted to run down her battery.

Kari gripped the door frame with one hand and hoisted herself inside. The space might be small, but it was home. Her home. There was comfort in that. She felt safer in the RV than in Connie's house.

Soft cries of annoyance came from outside as the others ran through the rain to join her.

"Hurry, hurry, hurry," Lorna insisted.

Kari turned to help them inside. The second she reached out her hand, her finger tingled, and a bright flash of light blinded her. The sound of the rain pelting the RV stopped. She knew before she opened her eyes what had happened.

Fuck.

Kari found herself standing alone at the bottom of the stairs in Connie's house. The storm continued outside, flashing through the windows. The box remained clutched in her hand.

What was it about this house? Why did it keep bringing her back? She looked up the stairs, waiting to see a flicker of light to indicate her mother had returned.

"Kari?"

"Kari, are you in here?"

The sound of her name came from the kitchen as the others entered the house.

"Yeah, I'm here," Kari answered.

"You just disappeared," Lorna said as she entered the hallway. "One second you were there, the next nothing. Like a ghost."

"Were you thinking of coming the house?" Vivien asked. They all gathered at the base of the stairs. Rain-drenched hair clung to their heads and clothes. "Did that activate your ability to transport in here?"

"Quite the opposite. I was thinking of how I

wanted to drive the RV out of town and never stop," Kari said. Even thinking of herself as having magical powers felt insane. She had proof of the supernatural, more every second, and still, her logical mind rebelled from the new truth. "I don't want to be here. I don't want to read Connie's creepy letters about freezing her eggs or go through her estate to deal with a chicken farm in the Deep South. What do I know about chickens? I don't want to be Queen of what remains of the squandered Grove Empire. I saw what having too much money turned my grandparents into. I feel like the house is holding me hostage. There is no way I'd transport myself here."

"All right," Lorna soothed. "Take a deep breath."

Kari inhaled sharply, but the air didn't help.

"Kidnapping houses. Well, this is definitely a new problem," Heather said. "Julia doesn't let things get boring."

"Better than killer clowns on the television telling us to run," Sue answered. "Or demons."

"Don't jinx us. It's early. We still don't know what's happening." Vivien walked down the hall, peeking in all the doorways.

"One thing at a time. We'll figure this out. First, we need towels." Lorna looked at the floor where they had tracked in water.

Kari pointed up the stairs. "Hall closet. Skinny door."

"Oh, no worries. I got the mess." Sue pointed at the floor. Nothing happened. She shook her hand a few times and then looked at her fingers. "That's weird."

"I'll get towels." Lorna ran up the stairs two at a time.

"What's up with the magic pointers?" Vivien asked.

"I don't..." Sue walked into the living room and flicked her hand a few times before sweeping her arm. "Nothing's happening. My powers didn't work on the boxes either."

"Hurry with the towels! It's freezing in here." Vivien rubbed her arms as her teeth began to chatter. "Something's wrong. I feel numb. This isn't right."

"I don't think it's that cold," Heather said.

"Are you sure you're not shivering because I'm picking up strong..." Vivien stepped close to Heather and leaned into her so that their faces nearly touched. "Nothing. I'm picking up nothing."

"I don't know what's happening. I can't clean anything," Sue said. "Or make a mess."

Vivien went to Sue and touched her face as she stared into her eyes. "Nothing. I don't understand. It's like you're empty. Less than a ghost."

Heather looked around. "I don't see any ghosts, which could mean something or just be my good fortune."

Vivien pushed past Sue and went to the kitchen. She came back wielding a knife.

Kari automatically took a step toward the door. "Oh, hold on now. Wait."

"Lorna, we need you," Vivien yelled, even as Lorna was carrying an armful of green paisley towels down the stairs.

"What happened?" Lorna tossed towels at Sue and Heather before handing one to Kari. "Is the ghost back?" When she started to give Vivien a towel, she drew back when she saw the knife. "Whoa."

Vivien put the tip of the blade to her hand and cut herself.

"No!" Kari gasped and instantly moved to stop her. She wrested the knife from Vivien's hand, and the woman didn't protest. "What are you doing?"

Vivien held her bloody hand toward Lorna. "Can you heal this?"

Lorna frowned. "Is that why you yelled for me? Do I look like a parlor monkey ready to perform? Kari already believes us. I'm not giving someone else your cut."

"A what?" Sue asked.

"She means grinder monkey, parlor trick," Heather translated under her breath as she dabbed at her wet hair.

"Do I look like a grinder monkey about to do parlor tricks?" Lorna asked, barely missing a beat.

"Just humor me. Move the cut to my right hand." Vivien pressed the corner of a towel into her wound to block the blood and then reached both hands toward Lorna.

"Fine." Lorna took Vivien by the wrists, closed her eyes for a few seconds, and then let go. "There."

Vivien turned her right hand over. It was unharmed. She then lifted the towel. The wound had not moved.

"What—no." Lorna frowned. "I..."

"Our magic's broken," Vivien said. "I can't feel any of you. I don't like this. It's not right."

"First aid kit?" Lorna asked.

"Check the bathroom," Kari pointed up the stairs.

Lorna ran back upstairs.

"I'll go to the theater and talk to Julia," Heather said. "I'll make her tell us what's going on."

"How? If your magic is broken and you can't see ghosts?" Sue asked.

"The séance book is in the car," Heather said. "Sue and Lorna, stay with Kari since she can't leave the house for very long, and in case her mother's ghost comes back. Viv, come with me. Julia loves talking to you, especially when she manifests in her younger form."

"We won't need the séance book. I'll just offer to bring up naked guy pictures on my phone again." Vivien tried to smile, but the look was strained.

"That'll do it," Heather agreed.

"Got it!" Lorna ran down the stairs breathing heavily. She tossed a roll of gauze at Vivien. "No antibiotic ointment, but I found that."

"Thanks." Heather handed the bloody towel to Lorna before working on bandaging her hand as she walked toward the door. "We'll be right back."

Heather squeezed Kari's arm briefly as she walked past to go out the front door.

"Thank—" Lightning cut off Kari's words, flashing so brightly it blinded her for a moment. When she could see again, Vivien and Heather had disappeared. The hard rain tried to come in through the front door but hit an invisible barrier and trailed down the opening like water over glass.

"Vivien? Heather?" Lorna called, rushing toward the entrance.

"Where did they go?" Sue asked, panic in her voice. "Viv! Heather!"

Kari stared at the door, unable to move. A strange feeling gnawed at her stomach and made it hard to breathe. Nothing made sense anymore.

"I can see the car, but they're just..." Lorna swayed on her feet. "They've vanished."

CHAPTER EIGHT

KARI STARED at the rain cascading down the invisible barrier. She clutched the box to her stomach as she tried to force a deep breath. Slowly, she reached toward the rain to see if her fingers would go through to the other side. "What is this?"

"Don't." Lorna grabbed her wrist to stop her. "We don't know what's happening."

"It started when we found that box," Sue said. "What's in it?"

Kari's grip tightened. She fingered the smooth edges where the lid should have been, but it didn't flip it open. Answers might be inside, but fear held her in its grasp and kept her from looking.

"She's right. The second you touched that box,

lightning struck." Lorna pushed the front door, so it swung shut over the barrier with a loud thud.

"Maybe we can sneak out a window?" Sue went into the living room and pulled back a curtain.

"What kind of Grandma Connie hell house ride was that?" Vivien's voice demanded from upstairs. Heather's muffled answer followed.

"Viv!" Lorna sprinted up the stairs two at a time. "Are you two all right? What happened? Where did you go?"

Sue and Kari followed her.

"Heather? Viv?" Lorna called. "Answer me."

"Here." Heather poked her head out of the haunted storage room. Her hair frizzed around her head. "We're fine. We're here."

"Speak for yourself. I think I have splinters in my ass from being shoved through that wall," Vivien grumbled. "Damn, Kari, did you not want us to leave? All you had to do was ask."

She clearly tried joking to lighten the mood. No one found it funny.

Kari clutched the box in her hands, working her fingers against it. "I swear, I don't think I'm doing this. I don't want to be in this house."

"Do you want me to try leaving?" Lorna asked.

"No," Heather said.

"Yes," Vivien answered at the same time. When Heather gave her a strange look, Vivien added, "You're the one always saying we need all the facts. Grandma Connie's Wild Ride didn't kill us. If anything, it'll spit her out here."

"Lorna, you don't have to," Heather said.

"If I think about it too much, I won't be able to force myself to try it. I'm going. If I make it out, I'll figure out a way to communicate with Julia." Before anyone could try to stop her, Lorna rushed down the stairs.

"Wait, I'm coming too." Sue made a strange noise of uncertainty before running after Lorna.

Kari heard the front door open and looked down the stairs just in time to see Lorna and Sue holding hands as they forced themselves through the front door. She turned her attention to the haunted room.

Lorna and Sue appeared as if stepping through the wall, still holding hands. Their eyes were closed, and Sue's cheeks puffed out as if she held her breath.

"Welcome back," Vivien stated wryly.

Lorna and Sue opened their eyes and slowly released their joined hands. Like Heather and Vivien, their hair had frizzed.

"I feel nauseous," Lorna said, touching her stomach. "That..." She gulped. "That wasn't fun."

"That was creepy as fuck." Sue took several deep breaths.

"I feel like the house left pieces inside me." Lorna brushed at her arms before shaking them violently as if to rid herself of spiders. "Soul splinters."

"So I guess this means no one can leave?" Sue looked to the others as if wanting them to deny her claim. No one did.

The sound of rain against the roof thumped steadily in the background, interrupted by loud bursts of thunder. One deafening crack caused them to jolt in surprise and look at the ceiling.

"How about you, Kari? Want to take a ride on the magic mystery transporter?" Vivien asked.

"I've been on it, no thanks," Kari refused. She had no idea what a soul splinter was, and she didn't want to find out. Strands of damp hair tickled her neck, and the wet clothes caused a chill to run over her entire length.

"I'll try calling Martin," Heather said, reaching into her pocket for her cell phone. She dialed and held it to her ear. "No signal."

Lorna and Sue tried their phones, and both shook their heads in denial.

"Nothing," Lorna said.

"Let's not panic. We can figure this out. It started

with that box," Heather said. "When you touched it, lightning struck."

"What's inside?" Vivien held her hand out as if to take the box from her.

Kari wrapped both hands around the box and hugged it to her stomach. The texture from the engravings pressed into her fingers. Another shiver worked over her. The wood felt fused to her as if she couldn't let go even if she wanted to.

"Kari?" Lorna asked. "Did you look inside?"

Kari shook her head. Feelings of stress and grief bubbled inside her—stress from magic and the funeral, grief for Connie but more for the mother she had never known. Even with these women standing around her offering friendship, she felt alone. Connie might have been sparse with love, but she had been family, a tie to someone else in the world. She felt tears trying to push their way from her eyes and held them back. "My mother wanted me to find this."

What if she didn't like what they discovered inside?

"The sooner you open it, the sooner we can figure a way out of here because sooner or later, we will run out of food," Vivien stated. "And I'm not about to turn into a news story in which I'm known for eating my—"

"Okay, easy, you're not taking it there," Heather

answered, giving Vivien a slight push as she stepped in front of her friend to block her from talking. "There's no reason to panic."

"There are like a thousand funeral casseroles in the freezer," Kari offered. "Help yourself."

"I don't feel right." Vivien fidgeted. She swayed on her feet and slapped her arms. "Nothing is coming at me. I'm in an emotional vacuum."

"Our magic isn't working." Heather turned to Vivien and placed hands on her shoulders to hold her still. "You only have your own emotions to feel right now."

"Well, that's not fun," Vivien said. "How do you survive like this? It's so...empty. I imagine this is what death feels like—walking, breathing death. Vacant with only my fear reflected back at me from the darkness. How do you only live in your own heads?"

"You're just not used to it," Lorna assured her. "Give yourself time."

"What if our magic doesn't come back?" Vivien leaned to look past Heather. "Kari, you need to open it. Please."

"I like not having my abilities," Heather admitted. "It's nice that no one is screaming in my ear for attention."

Kari tried to ease her hold on the box, but her

fingers wouldn't move. "My whole life, I never had anything that she gave me. I'm scared to look. What if it makes things worse? What if I don't want to know? What if Connie never told me things for a reason? What if—"

"Hey, now, that's not entirely true. Your mother gave you life," Lorna soothed.

Kari could tell Lorna was trying to be encouraging, but it didn't help.

"Getting pregnant is not the same as being a mother. The truth is I'll never know how my parents felt about me." Kari gave a derisive laugh. "Listen to me. I'm a grown-ass woman questioning if her parents wanted her, wondering how life would have been better had they lived. It's not like I was abandoned into social services and moved from foster home to group home to foster home. So what if Connie wasn't loving? I had everything I needed. We never lacked money or food. You'd think I'd be past this shit already. I promise you, despite what it might sound like, I don't just drive around in my RV all day feeling sorry for myself and wondering if Mommy and Daddy loved me."

"Oh, no, wait." Vivien lifted her hands. "Gah, I hate not sensing what people feel. How do you all...? Anyway, no. Just, no. There isn't an age limit on pain or hope or whatever it is you're feeling." She gave

Heather a lost look. "Help me out. What am I trying to say?"

"Life is complicated," Heather answered succinctly.

"Yes, complicated." Vivien nodded.

"You feel what you feel," Heather added. "No one should tell you that's wrong."

"Yes, that. No one should be told their feelings are wrong. I mean, unless they're a serial killer and then they're wrong, but that's not you, so...never mind." Vivien pointed at Heather. "What Heather's saying. Keep going."

"You really are lost without your gifts." Lorna patted Vivien on her shoulder.

Heather looked to where Kari's mother had materialized. The woman's eyes moved as if searching for signs of a ghost that would not manifest. "Whatever it is, whether it's Connie's, uh, Connie-ness, or your unresolved feelings about your parents, I think that's why you were given a ring. Everyone's greatest pain and fears are world-ending to them. For me, it was losing my son. For Vivien, it was losing a husband. For Lorna and Sue, it was various kinds of betrayal. For you, it's the parents you lost and the Connie who raised you."

"How was it being raised by Connie? Was she

always the way you describe?" Sue asked. "She sounds like a difficult woman to know. It might help to talk about her."

"You know that saying, if you don't have anything nice to say, don't say anything at all? I think that applies here." Kari tried to laugh, but none of this was funny.

"I was raised with that saying. I know it well," Lorna admitted. "I used to live by it. I liked being nice to people. I liked avoiding conflict. It's probably why I didn't call my ex out more on his crap. And whereas, in general, I think 'don't be an asshole' is great advice, I've also learned that sometimes unpleasant things need to be said. Sometimes those things need to be called out. Don't be mean just to be mean, but a lot of problems have festered in this world from nice people saying nothing. Then when their world explodes, they wonder how in the hell it happens."

"So you're saying what's happening now is my world exploding because I never confronted Connie?" Kari managed to ease her grip on the box.

"I think it might be part of the puzzle," Lorna said. "Either way, it can't hurt to talk about it. You might even feel better."

"The strangeness did start right around the time of the funeral." Kari had been filled with conflicting thoughts at the time. Drinking hadn't helped. "I was by the graveside the first time I transported back to this house and saw my mother."

Vivien's eyes fixed on Kari. She rubbed her arms. "Please, you have to open the box."

The woman's fear only appeared to worsen with the ticking seconds. The emotion seemed out of character compared to the Vivien she'd known so far.

Kari eased her grip. The lid had no lip to it, so she turned the box in her hands to figure out a way to get inside. Seeing a groove along the top hidden in the carvings, she pushed her thumbs firmly against it. The lid gave way and slid open. Her hands shook as she waited for something magical to happen—shooting lights, fairy sparkles, another ghost. The rain continued outside, but the thunder had eased.

The others leaned toward her, coming close to get a look inside. Kari held her breath and glanced around the room to ensure her mother hadn't reappeared.

"That's it?" Vivien frowned. "Dead weeds?"

Kari examined the contents of the box. Someone had bound dried plants into a little bundle.

"That's anti-climactic." Sue gestured her finger at the floor. "Still no magic."

"Weren't there a bunch of dried plants up here on the boxes?" Heather asked.

Kari nodded. "They smelled musty. The guys threw them away. I saw them in a trash bag earlier."

Kari picked up the bundle and handed it to Heather, along with a scrap of red material. At the bottom of the box was a leather-bound notebook covered with seeds. It had been wedged to fit the small space. She gently pried it free and shook the seeds into the box to contain them.

"Is this another séance book?" Lorna asked.

Kari handed the box to Vivien, who skimmed her fingers in the seeds to search for anything that might be buried within.

Kari opened the book a few pages in and read, "L. Wild blackberry root. Balmony. Poppyseed. Yew...?" She flipped a couple of pages, finding the same kind of lists. "This is Connie's handwriting. It looks like a recipe book."

"Great," Vivien drawled. "Gramma Connie's Creepy Cookbook."

"Is there a recipe for reversing imprisonment?" Lorna asked.

"It doesn't say what the lists are for. Just labels." Kari turned the pages as she read off the headings. "L. C. JW. P. K. D."

"JW? L?" Heather frowned.

"What is it?" Vivien asked.

"It wouldn't be the most secretive of codes, but they could be initials. I remember something about balmony being used in hexing people." Heather took the book from Kari to read it for herself. "JW. Julia Warrick. They used to be friends. L could be Lori. K for Kari."

"My grandfather was Clifford. C for Clifford," Kari added.

"Clifford," Heather stated as she looked for the page. She stopped and read, "Bitter orange. Foxglove. Guarana."

"Foxglove is digitalis. It can be poisonous, especially to people with heart conditions." Lorna took the book from Heather. "It's used to make heart medications, but those are regulated by big pharma. I believe it can also cause cardiovascular events in people." At Kari's questioning look, she added, "Helped with my son's science fair project when he was in high school. It had to do with nature being used as medicine. He didn't win. No one stood a chance against the battle robot."

"Guarana is a stimulant. I saw it advertised as being in a specialty soda at the coffee shop when I helped Jameson do inventory," Sue said. "I'd asked him about it. He said it's stronger than normal caffeine products."

"Stimulants and foxglove. That can't be a good combination." Vivien rubbed her arms. She looked more miserable with each passing minute.

Kari shook her head and automatically stepped back.

"What is it?" Lorna handed the book back to Heather.

"My grandfather died of a heart attack," Kari answered.

She heard Connie's voice in her head saying, *"You know all the stress you caused killed your grandfather. Sneaking him those cheeseburgers didn't help matters. He's dead because of you."*

"Are you saying Connie poisoned my grandfather?" Kari could barely form the words. "She wouldn't do that."

"Maybe it's a list of things to keep away from him? Or an herbal remedy to help him?" Lorna offered.

"He's dead because of you," the voice repeated.

"Connie didn't do herbal remedies." Kari took a deep, shaky breath. "When I told her I was taking garlic and fish oil for my cholesterol, she called it hippie hocus-pocus and told me to get real medicine from a doctor."

Heather continued to flip through the notebook. "It

looks like Connie was a little more into herbs than she let on."

"Are you sure it's hers?" Lorna asked.

"Yes, I..." Kari lifted a finger to indicate she needed a moment and quickly went to the guest room. Connie's letter remained on the bed where she'd left it. Grabbing it as her evidence, she brought it back to the others. "This is Connie's handwriting. She always prided herself on her penmanship."

Vivien placed the box of seeds on the floor and reached for the letter. She held it up so Heather could look at the writing and compare it to the notebook.

"Yep. It looks similar," Heather said. "Same loops and flourishes."

"Connie clearly had some secrets," Vivien added.

"So if L is for Lori, are you saying Connie hexed my mother?" Kari didn't want to have this conversation. The sound of rain continued on the roof, and the pounding became louder when she focused her attention on it. It heightened her anxiety. She felt trapped, just like in childhood, locked away in a room when her behavior had been unacceptable. "I don't want to be here. I want to go."

"Well, you are here, and we're here, and we need to figure out what's going on." Heather flicked the notebook toward Kari without letting go of it. She appeared irritated but quickly hid it. She held the book between them.

Kari slowly took the notebook from her and suppressed the urge to apologize.

Vivien held Connie's letter, her gaze moving over the page. "Wait, is this the frozen egg letter you started to tell us about earlier?"

"Yeah." Kari fingered the notebook but didn't open it. "I didn't finish reading it. She obviously wasn't in her right mind when she wrote it. I'm not sure why she thought I'd want her shriveled-up eggs as part of my inheritance."

"May I?" Vivien's gaze moved along the page even as she asked.

Kari almost refused and then shrugged. What did it matter? "Sure. Go ahead."

"Let's go downstairs," Lorna urged. "We'll sit, relax, and figure out this mystery while I put a casserole in the oven for all of us. Kari, any requests as to which one?"

"I don't care. I'm not hungry." Kari followed Lorna out of the room.

"You're still eating," Lorna put forth firmly, sounding very much like a sitcom mom laying down the law.

She heard footsteps behind her as they all went

down the stairs. The front door remained open from when Lorna and Sue tried to leave, and the rain continued to hit against the invisible barrier. Lorna bumped her foot against the door to swing it shut.

"I'll preheat the oven." Lorna made a beeline for the kitchen.

"She likes to feed people when she's nervous," Sue explained.

"Or happy," Heather added.

"Or awake." Vivien gave a small laugh. "Which is one of her most endearing qualities because she is an amazing cook."

"Lasagna or cheesy potato mystery?" Lorna called.

"Both," Vivien answered.

"I wish we had garlic bread." Even though she was loud enough to hear, it sounded like Lorna talked more to herself. The sound of the fridge opening and closing punctuated her musings. "Or at least a dinner salad or broccoli."

"Don't want the broccoli, just the carbs," Vivien yelled as she sat on the dingy couch with the letter. Heather sat next to her, sighing as she fell back against the couch and closed her eyes.

The décor was still dated, but the musty smell was gone, and the living room looked clean. The dark stains had disappeared from the worn carpet.

"Sue, thank you." Kari gestured at the cleaned room.

Sue nodded and sat next to Heather, leaving a chair for Kari.

"Oven's preheating." Lorna came in, saw no place to sit, and automatically turned back around. She came back seconds later with a dining room chair. "All right. I'm ready."

"Are you sure I can read this?" Vivien held up the letter.

"I'll tell you to stop if it gets too personal," Kari answered. "The truth is I'm hoping you can tell me it's not as bad as it sounded when I tried."

"*Kari,*" Vivien read aloud. "*You would not have been...*wow. She starts off with a bang, doesn't she?"

Heather opened her eyes and frowned as she leaned to read over Vivien's shoulder.

"Yep. That's Connie. All hearts and smiles," Kari muttered sarcastically.

"Not have been what?" Sue asked.

"*You would not have been my first choice in heirs,*" Heather continued where Vivien had stopped, "*but you are the only living relative, so taking care of the family properties falls on you.*"

Vivien resumed reading as Heather's voice trailed off, "*They tell me it's not legally advisable to demand you have a baby of proper breeding before you get your inheritance—"*

"Seriously, wow," Lorna whispered. "Proper breeding? I think you undersold the family trauma just a little."

"—which I think is bullshit," Vivien continued, *"but for the love of your family, we cannot let the bloodline die with you."* She looked at Kari. "Are you sure you want me to keep going?"

Somehow, seeing their appalled expressions made Kari feel better, like she wasn't crazy, like someone finally saw the truth. "I think you're about as far as I got with it before I had to stop."

Vivien turned back to the letter. *"Because I worry that you will never get your act together, I had some eggs cryogenically frozen and have interviewed surrogates to find the perfect candidate. I have also secured sperm donors of the highest quality."*

"And there it is," Kari said. "That's where I stopped reading."

"Does she want you to raise your own aunt?" Heather asked.

"It's insane, all of it." Kari pinched the bridge of her nose in an attempt to stop an oncoming headache. "It's dated six years ago, so Connie was in her seventies when she wrote that to me, well through menopause.

Unless she did it when I was a kid, I don't know how this is even an option."

"Do eggs last that long frozen?" Sue asked. "I mean, I'd think there has to be a viability issue with the popsicles after thirty to forty years."

"I'd look it up on my phone, but..." Lorna let the words trail off.

"Popsicles?" Heather chuckled. "Is that a medical term, Doctor?"

Sue gestured helplessly. "Don't they freeze them in canisters or something? That's what it looks like in movies. Giant metal containers inside even bigger metal containers with nitrogen."

"Was this movie on the science fiction channel?" Heather teased. "Were they alien babies?"

Kari didn't think it would be possible, but the idea of alien Connie babies in test tubes made her laugh. She covered her mouth as her shoulders began to shake, but once it started, it was difficult to stop. She leaned over her lap.

"Is she laughing or crying?" Vivien asked. "I can't tell."

"I think laughing?" Sue said.

"Hold that thought. Oven should be ready. I'll put the casseroles in." Lorna left for the kitchen, pausing long enough to give Kari a tiny pat on her back.

"Kari, you good?" Vivien asked.

Kari heard Lorna banging around as she put the food in the oven. She laughed harder as she sat back in her chair. "Alien babies."

"Did we break her?" Heather studied her face.

"Looks like it." Vivien pushed up from the couch. "Lorna, bring glasses. I'm getting the wine."

Kari tried to catch her breath as her eyes teared from the laughter. "It's just, the funeral, and lawyer, and this crappy house, and that letter, and everything. It's...it's..."

"Funny?" Sue didn't sound convinced.

"It's so much," Kari finished, wiping her eyes. "It's not funny. I don't know why I'm laughing. Maybe I'm hysterical. It's just if I don't laugh, I'll scream."

"Hey, we already said you don't have to apologize for how you feel." Vivien rejoined them. She handed the bottle to Heather.

Lorna returned carrying empty water glasses and a wine opener. She gave the corkscrew to Heather and set the glasses on the coffee table. "They should be ready in thirty-five, forty minutes."

"Where were we?" Heather prompted as she opened the bottle.

Vivien resumed reading, "*I hope you realize you left me little choice in the matter. What else was I to do?*

Our family lines can't die out. The Groves and the Alcotts are both proud, important families, and that importance must carry on."

"Alcott is her maiden name," Kari interjected.

"I have waited patiently for you to find a suitable husband, but your quaint notion that marriage is based on love is both pedestrian and narrow-minded. Love destroys empires."

"Yep, we're going to need to summon Connie back. I have a couple of choice words for her." Lorna waited as Heather poured wine in the glasses before handing them out.

"Yeah," Kari drawled wryly as she looked around the neglected living room. She shook her head when Lorna offered her a glass. "Look at the great Alcott-Grove empire. Behold and be jealous. I'm not trying to be an ass about what I inherited. A few million is nothing to sneeze at, but Connie always made it sound like she was royalty rich."

"I can't fully blame you for this," Vivien continued. *"Your mother did not set a very good example for you with her choices. I did my best by you, as you are, after all, my heir."*

Kari tried to ignore the fear and guilt knotted in her chest as Vivien continued to read. These were not new insults, but to hear them said by someone else caused those old feelings of embarrassment and inadequacy to form inside her. She had never been enough for Connie, and the woman's resentment permeated every second of her life.

"For these reasons, I know you'll understand the wisdom of my decisions and why I waited to tell you about your..." Vivien hesitated. Her eyes lifted to Kari, and she said, "You have a daughter."

"So she does want me to raise my aunt as my kid?" Kari stood and took the letter from Vivien. She paced out of the living room and down the hall next to the stairway as she read.

...I waited to tell you about your daughter. She was born this morning and thankfully looks like my side of the family. I have named her Constance. A van is no place to raise a child, but now with your inheritance, you are financially secure enough for home ownership. It is time you took your responsibilities seriously.

"Constance?" Kari whispered. She felt the hallway walls close in on her. She wasn't the last member of the Grove family. There was a baby—no, a child—named after her grandmother, somewhere out in the world.

Should anything happen to the child, Dr. Spitz has your remaining harvested eggs in stock from the same hospital where you received your appendectomy. He's located in the new Alcott-Grove fertility wing and is familiar with the privacy requirements of your file. Don't cause one of your scenes if you call them. I had legal medical power of attorney while you were in surgery, and any protests at this point would only cause embarrassment.

"Kari?" Lorna asked from the doorway.

Kari was too stunned to say anything but the bizarre truth. "Connie stole my eggs when I had an emergency appendectomy seven years ago, used them in a surrogate she impregnated with donor sperm, and now I have a six-year-old kid somewhere."

"What?" Heather and Sue asked in unison. They both brushed past Lorna to stand near the bottom of the stairs.

Vivien joined them, walking and pouring a large amount of wine into a glass. She offered it to Kari. "Want this?"

Kari nodded and took a big drink. The woodsy flavor of the merlot wasn't her favorite, but at the moment, she didn't care. The overpowering taste made her gulp several deep breaths before she could manage, "What the hell, Connie?"

"This can't be real," Sue said. "How is it even possible?"

Kari turned back to finish the letter, wishing she could unread the damned thing.

The lawyer will be instructed to give you a list of miscellaneous assets that are not included in the main family trust. Answers you need will be in there. All of it must stay in the family. Don't screw this up. C.

"What the hell, Connie?" Kari suppressed a scream.

"May I?" Vivien held out her hand.

Kari gave the letter to Vivien. "Go ahead. Finish reading it."

As Vivien read the remainder of the letter out loud, Kari went to find the manila envelope from the lawyers where she'd left it in the dining room before they went out to look through the bricks. Buried in the legal documents was much of what she'd seen before—stocks in various companies, property deeds, furniture store, the Freewild house, the damned chickens, but nothing about a mysterious child begot of stolen eggs.

If there were answers in the papers, she didn't see them. There were no hints as to where Connie had hidden Constance.

Kari dropped the papers. A few slid over the table and fluttered onto the floor. She touched her stomach and sank to her knees. Her forehead pressed into the back of a chair.

"Kari?" Heather knelt next to her.

"Complications," Kari whispered.

"Yes, it's complicated," Heather agreed.

"They told me after my surgery that there had been minor complications, and that's why it took longer than expected," Kari recalled.

Heather waited patiently for Kari to collect her thoughts.

"I don't know how I'm supposed to feel about this." A tear slipped down her cheek, and she swiped at it. She took several deep breaths, having a hard time steadying herself. "I'm so...so..."

"Violated?" Heather suggested.

"Yeah, yeah." Kari nodded. "Violated. Invaded. Angry. I'm *so* angry, and the one person I want to tear a new asshole is dead."

Heather nodded.

"This must be what guys feel like when they suddenly discover they're a father and no one told them. What am I going to do with a child? I live in an RV. You can't raise a kid on the road, can you?" Kari banged her head against the chair a few times in frustration. "Oh, and that poor girl. I wouldn't wish Connie's parenting on anyone. Who knows what kind of damage has been done? I should have read that letter when I got it. I didn't realize it was this. I thought Connie wanted to insult me one last time and guilt me into being her surrogate. Never, in a million years, would I suspect she was capable of this."

Heather slipped her arm around Kari and gently pulled her to her feet before urging her to sit in the chair. She then began gathering the fallen papers.

When Heather placed the papers on the table, Kari grabbed her arm. "What if the kid hates me?"

"What if she ends up being the best thing you never knew you wanted?" Heather countered as she took a seat next to her. "I get you've been thrown for several loops and deserve time to process, but at the end of the day, you have a daughter, and she's six. As much as you didn't ask for this, neither did Constance. I'm not saying you have to raise her. She may be with parents who love her, and they're the best thing for her. I can't make that call for you. Parenting isn't always about biological matches. Only you know what you are willing to do and sacrifice. But you should meet her and help her if she needs it."

Kari tried to answer, but she didn't know what to say. Her emotions were all over the place. "I'm not going—"

"Well, you were worried that your pain wasn't deep enough or your story strange enough to be part of the Julia Warrick ring club," Vivien said, joining them at the table. "I think this qualifies you for a lifetime membership. I also think you should sue that doctor for all kinds of medical malpractice, possibly assault, and not just the doctor. You should sue everyone in that operating room and the hospital administration, and you should close that whole damn fertility wing. A medical power of attorney would not give Connie the right to have your eggs harvested. You say the word, and I'll help you find a lawyer that will have you owning that entire hospital by the end of the year."

Sue entered carrying plates and silverware. She started placing them on the table. "Lorna said the casseroles are almost heated enough to eat."

Kari didn't want to think about food or malpractice suits, for that matter. Suing the hospital would not change the reality of her life. If anything, it would only make her family tragedy all the more publicly embarrassing. She'd become the punchline of late-night talk show jokes and social media memes. Not to mention what it would do to the kid's life if this were known.

"Do you want me to contact a lawyer?" Vivien asked.

"I need time to think. I think we need to séance Connie." Kari said at length. "You said we can do that, right? I want to make her face me, face what she's done. I want her to tell me why she thought this was all right."

She looked at her hands, remembering the feel of the pillow, and silently added, *I need her to tell me I didn't hurt her that last day in her room.*

Vivien leaned over and patted her hand. "Atta girl."

CHAPTER NINE

A LOUD BANGING noise woke Kari from a dead sleep. The heavy fog of wine and grief disoriented her, and she took a few seconds to register she'd slept on the couch. Her attention went to the patched ceiling. Why were the workers here?

Footsteps entered the house, and she sat up just in time to see a man dressed in work overalls storm past her down the hall toward the kitchen, yelling, "Heather? Heather, are you in here?"

A second man followed the blur of the first and paused at the bottom of the stairs to look up. He had short dark hair with hints of gray at the temples and wore a knitted cardigan. He didn't look like he belonged on a construction job. "Viv?"

"Troy?" Vivien appeared on the stairs. Her steps

were stunted as if she had just woken up. Half yawning, half talking, she asked, "What are you guys doing here?"

"I was at the house looking for you after you missed our date, and Martin came by. He said Jan called him. She had received a message, and we came looking for you." Troy pulled Vivien against him. "We were so worried."

"Is Heather with you?" The first man reappeared in the doorway.

"Hi, Martin. She's upstairs," Vivien answered. Martin brushed past her and ran up the stairs. "First bedroom on the left."

Kari watched them through the doorway. Since they'd been trapped in the house, Vivien and Heather had slept in Connie's old room, and Sue and Lorna had taken the guest room.

Kari threw the blanket off her legs and went to look at the front door. The storm was over and early morning light shone on the porch.

"Kari, I'd like you to meet Troy." Vivien paused to give her boyfriend a quick kiss.

Kari nodded weakly at the man and walked toward the open door. "Can we leave?"

She stepped through the threshold into the

sunlight. When she stood on the porch, she took a deep breath of relief.

"Looks like it." Vivien joined her. "Thank goodness. If the rest of the casseroles are like that mystery meal we had last night, I don't think my system could survive it."

"I can assume this is one of your," Troy paused as if searching for diplomatic phrasing, "*things*."

"Yep. The house kidnapped us last night, and we couldn't leave or call out," Vivien said.

"Sounds about right." Troy shook his head.

"How did you know where to find us?" Vivien asked.

"Uh?" He glanced at Kari.

"She's one of us." Vivien nodded at Kari. "Show him the ring."

Kari lifted her hand.

"Grandma Julia strikes again." Troy sighed. "Jan said a dead woman named Muffy told her you were all trapped in here. The ghost was weak, so she didn't have a lot of details, only that you were trapped in a storm, which didn't make sense because there wasn't a storm."

Kari looked at the ground. After the rain locking them inside, the ground should have been soaked. The dirt was completely dry.

"Dammit," Vivien grumbled.

"What?" Troy asked.

Vivien frowned. "That means I'm going to have to be nice to Muffy later."

"House kidnapped? Is that why it looked like plastic wrap was over the door when we came up the porch?" Troy asked.

"It did? You could see it?" Kari studied the door. No part of her wanted to walk back into the house.

Troy nodded. "It disappeared when Martin pushed his way inside. Well, more like it melted into thin air. I don't know. It was magic-y weird."

"Ah, so you came to rescue me?" Vivien gave Troy a playful smile as she pinched his cheeks. "That's my big hero knight in shining armor."

"I'd jump into a volcano if I thought it would save you from danger, my lady," Troy said. "But, alas, you're the last person who I'd think needs rescuing. I almost feel sorry for danger if it comes up against you."

"Oh, thank goodness, my magic is back. I can feel what you're feeling." When Vivien smiled, her entire being changed. "You say the sweetest things, Troy, and you're acting tough, but you were worried about me."

"My abilities are back, too," Heather said from the doorway. Her tone was less enthusiastic. She gave a halfhearted gesture toward the street and turned her eyes downward. "Ghost dandy in a top hat."

To Kari, the street looked empty.

"Kari, I'd like you to meet Martin." Heather introduced her to the man in work overalls.

"Nice to meet you, Martin," Kari said. Then realizing she hadn't exactly greeted Troy warmly, she added, "And you, Troy."

"Sorry about barging into your home uninvited," Martin answered. "The message we got sounded like you ladies were in serious trouble."

"It's not my house...well, I guess technically it is, but not really." Kari briefly wondered what the consequences would be if she set the place on fire. If there was no house to go to, maybe it couldn't drag her back.

"Whatever you're thinking, you know it's not right," Vivien said to Kari. Then smiling, she said, "I'm back. I can sense you. Quick, think about something else."

Kari's thoughts instantly turned to the letter and her daughter.

"Oh." Vivien's expression fell. "I'm sorry. I should have kept my mouth shut."

Lorna and Sue joined them on the porch.

"Thank goodness the storm is over." Sue looked around the dry yard and frowned as she too recognized the anomaly.

"I'm going to call Jan and let her know everything's

all right. She's at a slumber party, but I'm sure she's been frantic since calling to tell me Muffy had a message that you were in danger." Martin pulled out his phone and stepped toward the vehicles.

"I want to talk to her when you're done," Heather said. "I'd promised to text her last night, and I wasn't able to."

"How can I help?" Troy asked.

"Don't you have to teach an online class this morning?" Vivien inquired.

"Canceled it when Martin told me what was going on," Troy answered. "Trust me. The students won't miss my fascinating lecture on synthetic division."

"It's so sexy when you talk math nerd." Vivien chuckled, kissing him.

That made sense. Troy had that college professor look about him.

"Polynomial," Troy whispered. Vivien laughed.

"Get a room, you two," Lorna teased, turning to go back into the house.

"Wait." Kari put her arm up to stop her. "What if you can't get back out?"

Lorna took Kari's hand and gently lowered her arm. "Then you know where to find me."

Lorna went inside. Sue walked to the edge of the porch and stared at the lawn. Heather spoke on the phone by the cars as Martin stood next to her, his arm around her shoulders. Vivien and Troy talked amongst themselves. Vivien chuckled softly at something he whispered.

Kari glanced inside the opened front door, not wanting to step back into the house. She turned to join Sue by the edge of the porch. Angel's truck appeared down the street, heading toward the house...

White light flashed, and she automatically lifted her arms as if to stop the teleportation. It didn't work.

CHAPTER TEN

WHEN THE LIGHT FADED, Kari stood alone in the haunted storage room. She automatically darted for the door. Instinct told her to run. The knob pulled from her grasp as an invisible force slammed the door shut.

Kari cried out in fright. Her hands shook as she tried to turn the knob. She couldn't be trapped with more family secrets. Not again. Even with the broken frame, the door wouldn't budge.

Fwap-fwap-fwap...

"No," Kari whispered. She'd had about all the supernatural she could stand. She weakly kept tugging on the knob. Projector light flickered from behind her.

...fwap-fwap-fwap...

"No," she said louder, slapping the flat of her hand against the wood. "Let me go!"

...fwap-fwap-fwap...

Kari fell against the door, her forehead thumping on the wood as she refused to turn around.

"Mom, I'm sorry. I can't handle any more family secrets. Connie's letter says I have a daughter. The notebook we found looks like she might have killed my grandfather. You gave me a ring that does weird things I don't understand. This house won't let me go—or you, or Connie, or whatever it is that keeps forcing me back. And I have enough human problems to figure out with the inheritance without adding paranormal ones. Apparently, I freaking own chickens now, and—"

...fwap-fwap-fwap...

The sound became louder and faster.

"Mom. *Lori*, I don't want—"

...fwap-fwap-fwap...

It became louder still as if her mother screamed at her from beyond the grave.

"Fine! Tell me." Kari spun to face the ghost. The action caused dizziness, and she swayed before righting herself.

The storage room disappeared, replaced by an open field. The *fwap-fwap* of the projector faded into a faraway laugh. Her mother no longer looked 2D as she twirled in circles. Flowers dotted the tall, wind-rustled grasses, but the air felt still and smelled like the musty storage room. She saw the bright sunlight but couldn't feel its warmth.

The edges of the scenery were blurred as if the lost details were plucked from the depths of someone's memory. Her mother smiled in her direction and pointed at the ground. Kari turned her attention to an orange kitten flicking its paws at a blade of grass.

"Look. He reminds me of you," Lori said.

Kari stiffened to hear her voice.

Her mother leaned over the kitten.

"Feisty?" a man answered from behind her. Kari turned, but the man stood beyond the clear edges and was more of a dark impression of a tall, slender shape.

"Cute and fluffy," Lori corrected. "Put that camera down."

The image froze with her mother's hand mid-pet and the kitten's mouth open.

"I don't understand?" Kari said to the image. "You were pointing at a kitten?"

The image flickered...

...*fwap-fwap-fwap*...

...and then faded.

"That's what you needed to tell me so badly? Cute and fluffy?" Kari frowned. Instead of the storage room, a new memory appeared.

"What are you doing? You can't record this." Her

mother's laugh forced Kari's attention to turn. Lori waited on a twin-sized bed. Her hair had been permed and teased, a style popular in the eighties. She sat back on her ankles with her bare knees poking out from under her oversized t-shirt. The shirt had a dinosaur on the front. Behind her on a wall was a pennant with the letters FCHS on it, which seemed out of place next to posters for bands like Siouxsie and the Banshees and the Ramones. Movie theater ticket stubs had been pinned between them.

"What do you think I'm recording?" the male voice asked with a laugh.

"You know." Lori blushed and glanced at the bed. "Us. Together."

Kari tried to follow her mother's gaze, but again the cameraman stood beyond the range of clarity.

"I'm hunting T-Rex in the wild." The man's tone shifted as if narrating a nature documentary. "The feisty female of the species—"

"Cute and fluffy," Lori corrected, pulling her elbows into the sleeves of her shirt to mimic the short arms of a dinosaur. She gave a tiny little roar and worked her hands like claws.

"The little-known cute and fluffy variety of T-Rex is notorious for sneaking out of her parents' house, even when grounded, and never doing as she's told," the man stated. "Total anarchy."

"That's to escape the monstrous Connie-saurus, the most dangerous of all dried-up fossils." Lori looked incredibly happy and young and in love. It was there in her smiling eyes, in the playful movements of her fake dinosaur hands, in the sound of her laugh. "She actually tried locking me in my room this time."

"The fluffy T-Rex can also pick locks," the man said.

"Thanks to lessons from the fluffy T-Rex's boyfriend." Lori's gaze shifted, and her expression fell. She pushed her elbows free of the sleeves and sat on the bed cross-legged. "You know next time she'll probably try to chain me to the bed. She's getting worse. I swear she's trying to mind-control me. She put something in my food and then did a weird incantation under her breath over dinner last night."

"Did she hide broccoli in your cheese, little girl?" he teased.

"Shut up, I'm serious."

"Connie might be a bitch, but she's no witch," the man said. "She can't mind-control you. She just wants you to think that. All parental units do."

"You don't know what I've seen. Some lady from Louisiana brought her a bunch of stuff this morning,"

Lori said. "They were talking about binding living spirits."

"She's a bitch and a kook," the man corrected.

"How can you not believe? She was best friends with Julia Warrick before they had a falling out," Lori insisted.

"*Oooo*," the man wavered as he pretended to be a ghost. "The witch of Freewild Cove. It must be true then."

"You don't know. You haven't seen what I've seen. The second I graduate, I'm out of here. I'll go somewhere she'll never think to look for me," Lori said. "I'll change my name."

Kari remembered that feeling well, the need to escape. In fact, she had. She'd started running and hadn't stopped.

"Where can you go that the Alcott-Grove fortune can't find you?" the man asked.

"Hong Kong. Bali. Australia?" Lori's face lit up with the possibilities of her dreams.

"Chicago," the man suggested. "It'd be a lot cheaper. I should be able to save enough for a couple of bus tickets."

"Chicago?" Lori wrinkled her nose. "What would I do in Chicago?"

"Be my groupie. I have an uncle there. He can give

us a place to stay while I work on my music."

Chicago.

Kari turned her attention from her mother to the man. The blurred image remained out of focus, but she stared at him for any hint of his face. She stepped closer to him, desperate for any glimpse. "Dad?"

He didn't hear her, didn't react to her presence. Neither of them did.

"We?" Lori stood from the bed.

"After you marry me, of course," he said.

Lori laughed. "Is that a proposal, Mr. Washington?"

Mr. Washington.

She had a name. Her father's last name was Washington.

"Foregone conclusion," her father answered. "You know you can't live without me, Lori Grove. And you know I can't live without you. Besides, you said you wanted to change your name."

The man stepped forward and set something down on what appeared to be a dresser. He came halfway into focus. Kari stared up at him, willing him to glance down just once to see her. She never imagined her father would be so tall.

Or that he'd be rocking a shaggy black mohawk, eyeliner, and a studded wristband and collar.

Oh, Connie would have hated this pairing. She wouldn't have wanted her daughter to date a punk rocker with holey t-shirts and ripped jeans, let alone marry him and have his baby.

Kari had suspected there was something about her father Connie hated but seeing this confirmed the reasons behind her grandmother's endlessly snide comments. Connie wouldn't have outright said it, but the bias had been there. Mr. Washington would have been so far beneath their social standing and an intolerable family embarrassment. No wonder Lori felt the need to run away.

Her parents started to kiss. Kari made a weak noise, hoping she wasn't about to witness her own conception.

Lori pushed him away and fell back onto the bed. "Not on camera."

Her father laughed. Even as he stood up to go back to the camera, he said, "It's for posterity. We can watch it when we're old."

"You mean to traumatize the grandkids after we—" Lori began.

The scene froze as it had with the kitten. The blurred image of her father held the camera in his hands, presumably shutting it off. Lori lay on the bed, grinning. Everything about her expression said she was in love. They had been so young, too young to die so tragically.

"You had so many plans," Kari whispered to the pair. "Chicago, marriage, grandkids..."

Kari realized that would have been her life, too. She could have spent her childhood waking up to that smile instead of the stern face of whatever underpaid nanny Connie had hired.

"I don't know why I'm seeing this, but if I can change the past..." Kari approached her mother. "Something goes wrong with my delivery. Get to a doctor sooner and demand all the tests they have. And don't let Dad leave your side that day. He needs to watch out for—"

...fwap-fwap-fwap-fwap...

The image flickered and faded, as did the sound of the phantom projector.

"No!" Kari yelled.

"Kari?" Heather appeared in the doorway. "What happened?"

Kari brushed a tear from her cheek. "Washington."

The name escaped her lips as if she were afraid that she would somehow forget it.

"Washington?" Heather frowned.

"That was my father's last name. I saw him. I saw..." Kari gestured helplessly to where she'd first seen her mother. "Her. I saw my mother again. She was afraid Connie was trying to bind a living spirit or something and was putting strange things in her food."

"I heard a scream. Is everything all right up here?" Angel appeared behind Heather.

"Yeah," Kari turned and swiped at her eyes to stop the tears that threatened to fall. "Yeah, I just... Yeah."

"It's one of those things," Heather said.

"Oh." Angel nodded as if he understood. "I'm sorry to hear of your troubles. You're in good hands, though."

"You know?" Kari studied him.

"These ladies helped my mother after my aunt Mariana died. She kept hiding my mother's jewelry. They were family heirlooms that the two of them used to bicker over. I was there when they did a séance," he said. "I suspected something otherworldly might be happening to you. Heather asked me to keep an eye out while we were here working. Is it your grandmother?"

Kari wasn't sure how to answer.

"We're not sure yet," Heather said. "It's a complicated matter."

"I imagine it always is when dealing with the afterlife." Angel lifted his hand as if to touch Kari's shoulder but then dropped it. Some people just had goodness in them. Angel was one of those people. There was a kindness in him that showed in each word and gesture.

"I know a little bit about what you're going through if you'd ever like to talk about it."

Kari doubted his aunt who passed away was anything like Connie. "Thank you."

"Or if you just want to go have coffee and hang out sometime," he said.

"Thank you," Kari answered, distracted. She wondered if the house would make her disappear in public when people were watching.

"Or, you know, dinner?" He gave her a hesitant smile.

Kari nodded. She'd been in the bookstore, which was technically public, but she'd also been alone in the store at the time, so no one saw where she went. Well, Ace, but she doubted the cat would tell anyone.

Heather softly cleared her throat and moved closer. She whispered, "Date."

Kari blinked rapidly in surprise as she came out of her deep thoughts. "Date? Oh, dinner, date, yes. Sorry. I mean, maybe." She looked at a confused Angel, who seemed torn between laughter and some other emotion she couldn't quite name. Without careful considera-tion, she found herself taking a deep breath and answering, "Yes. I'd like that. Sometime. Yes. Thank you."

"Good." He nodded toward the repaired floor. His

smile widened. "I'm going to finish prepping the living room ceiling for paint."

When Angel left, Kari hit the palm of her hand to her head. "Wow. I'm a complete idiot. Did that look as bad as I think it was?"

"Not the smoothest social transaction I've ever seen." Heather chuckled. "But hey, he's a nice guy and cute. You could do worse. I think you are allowed a little leniency considering all you have going on."

Kari closed her eyes and took a deep breath. Angel was much more than cute. From that first moment she saw him standing at the bottom of the stairs she'd been attracted to him. Until now, she wasn't sure if he felt the same way.

Her feelings scattered all around like mismatched pieces of several puzzles not meant to fit together. So many thoughts wanted her attention that a love life didn't stand a chance at moving to the forefront. Until she fixed her life, a boyfriend would never stand a chance.

"I need to find out more about my father. Maybe he has family in the area," Kari said.

"You mean, maybe you have family in the area?" Heather asserted.

Family.

Kari felt a tremor of excitement and fear work

through her. Connie might not be her last relative. "He mentioned an uncle in Chicago, but I think they went to school here. I saw one of those cloth, sports, banner pennant things on the wall that read FCHS."

"Freewild Cove High School." Heather pulled out her phone. "Maybe we can find out something from the yearbook. I know Gretchen over at the school. She's the librarian. They should have copies of all the yearbooks. I'll give her a call."

"She would have graduated around nineteen-eighty to eighty-one," Kari said.

"I'll see if we can borrow nineteen-seventy-five to eighty-two just to cover our bases." Heather began typing on her phone. "If you're up for it, we want to head over to the theater to do a séance and talk to Julia. Maybe she can tell us something about Connie and that notebook."

"But what if I...?" Kari looked around.

"You won't be driving, and if you disappear, we know where to find you." Heather motioned that Kari should follow. "I think it's worth a shot."

"Okay." Kari nodded and moved to go downstairs.

"You should probably put some shoes on first, though," Heather said.

Kari glanced at her dirty bare feet. "Any chance I would have time for a quick shower?"

CHAPTER ELEVEN

AFTER ALL THE talk about séances and magic, Kari expected Warrick Theater to be some mystical place. Instead, she found an old building with art deco light fixtures and panels on the ceiling. The gold and burgundy sponge-painted walls reminded her of Connie's home décor in the early nineties. The jewel tones had been popular with her grandmother's crowd back then.

Kari looked around the lobby. She wondered if she should try to hide from view. The glass security doors automatically locked behind her, but she heard the occasional car driving down Main Street. She only hoped if she transported out of there, no one would see her from the road.

Kari's hair had air-dried, and she saw the mess of

brown curls in the window reflection. Her first instinct was to smooth them back and make herself "presentable." Connie's word, not hers. Kari didn't touch her hair.

Lorna went behind a concessions stand and pulled out several boxes of candy. She lobbed one toward Vivien. "Fuel up."

"Aye, aye, Captain," Vivien answered with a small salute.

Heather caught a box against her chest and told Kari, "You'll want the sugar."

Kari caught a box Lorna tossed at her.

"Did you read the plaque outside about Julia?" Lorna asked.

Kari shook her head in denial.

"Kari was too busy keeping her head down." Vivien paused to drop a couple of pieces of candy into her mouth. Chewing a little as she talked, she added, "Afraid she'd disappear off the sidewalk."

"Sounds like one of those stories in those tabloid papers Julia liked to read," Heather said. "The Disappearing Woman of Freewild Cove. Right next to alien abductions and the lady who married her iguana."

Lorna hooked Kari's arm and guided her toward the curtains next to the concessions. The thick velvet hung over the auditorium's entryway. "Julia is a fascinating character. You ever watch those bootlegger movies?"

"Sure," Kari answered. They passed through the curtains to the theater's seating area. About a hundred chairs were divided by two aisles, which led to a black-painted stage and movie screen.

Lorna released Kari's arm. "That's Julia."

Kari stiffened, looking around. She didn't see a ghost. "Where?"

"No, I mean she's like those movies. Julia ran a bootlegger ring. It's how she made all her money." Lorna motioned for her to keep walking. "She was also a pot farmer and burlesque dancer."

"She's my hero," Vivien inserted. "That woman did not squander her time on Earth."

"Julia also owned a bunch of properties here in town. She built this theater." Lorna led the way down the aisle to the stage. "She was a big name in the Spiritualist movement. She used to host séances here, onstage. People would come from all over the country to watch her contact the dead. We found a book listing her séances, the results, how many chickens she was paid for each one, like an accountant's ledger. Besides that, the book also taught us how to contact the dead. That's what we're going to show you today."

Having seen a movie poster for a nineteen-seventies not-so-classic film outside, Kari guessed the theater now catered to a different audience.

"It wasn't always chickens," Vivien said. "Sometimes it was root vegetables."

"It was the Great Depression," Heather explained as she crossed a row to the other aisle. "People traded what they could afford to give. Julia would have done readings for free, and did, but for a lot of people, it was a matter of pride."

"I'm trying to get William to write a book about her life." Lorna stopped about halfway down. "He says he doesn't want to write about his grandma's burlesque days."

"You should do it yourself," Heather said. "With your finder power, you'll be able to uncover all her secrets."

Heather tripped as if pushed from behind. She caught her hand on a seat and laughed.

"Julia wants editorial rights," Heather stated with a glance over her shoulder. "And for you to use words like scandalous when you talk about her burlesque days. I'm paraphrasing, but she says she wants it to be shocking, and she refuses to be remembered as boring."

"Oh, good, she's here." Vivien nodded toward Kari in what was supposed to be a reassuring gesture. "Julia manifests stronger here. So much of her psychic energy imprinted on this place in life."

Kari stared behind Heather, still trying to discover some kind of hint that a ghost was there. She saw nothing abnormal. A chill ran down her back.

"This theater is the only place I felt normal as a kid." Heather looked around as if seeing things that the rest of them couldn't, but Kari wasn't sure whether they were ghosts or memories. "Grandma Julia always understood me in a way my mother never could. I feel her here, even when I can't see her."

"I like living here." Sue pointed toward the ceiling. "My apartment is upstairs. Having Julia down here makes me feel safe like I have my own personal supernatural security guard. I imagine she keeps the pervert ghosts from watching me in the bathroom."

"She says she will," Heather answered, "but wants me to tell you that there aren't any lurkers in her theater."

"Let's set up," Vivien said.

"I'll get the supplies from the office. New candles arrived last week." Lorna ran back up the aisle. "Sue, give me a hand?"

"Sure thing." Sue followed Lorna as she left the auditorium.

Kari glanced around nervously, not seeing any

ghosts. She watched Heather's eyes move down a row of seats only to pause a few times. The woman said something, but her voice was too low to hear.

Vivien turned her back to the stage and hopped to sit on the edge. She slid backward and lifted her legs up before standing. "Join me, Kari."

Kari walked down the aisle, more interested in watching Heather gesture at an empty seat. No matter how hard she strained her vision, Kari couldn't see anyone on the other side of that conversation. When she neared the stage, she went to the steps instead of following Vivien's method of jumping up.

"How do you deal with this?" Kari asked, nodding at Heather. "You can't see them, but they're there."

Vivien smiled. She seemed more at ease now she had her abilities back. "The females in my family have always had the gift, so I grew up knowing there was more beyond what I see. It's never bothered me. I don't look at it as something I have to deal with. It just is. Like breathing."

"So all the women in your family are psychic?" Kari asked.

Vivien directed her attention toward the empty seats and then back again. "It's called clairsentient, which is a fancy way of saying we feel what other people are feeling and understand why they might be feeling that way. And claircognizant because we just kind of know if something is real or not, without a way to explain how we know."

Vivien went to the edge of the stage as Lorna came down the aisle carrying a canvas bag. Lorna handed it over before going to the stairs.

"How did you...? I mean, growing up, did...?" Kari thought it best not to finish the line of thought. It might be rude to ask if people thought she was weird as a child.

"It's all right," Vivien said. "You don't have to worry about offending me."

Sue appeared through the curtains with a box. "I had chocolate cake donuts upstairs."

Vivien placed the bag on the floor and pulled out a large bundle of material.

"My ancestors were carnies." Vivien placed an object wrapped in blue cloth on the stage floor. She began peeling back the fabric as if it was the most reverent of tasks. "They read tarot cards on the carnival circuit, did future predictions, that sort of thing. I don't think my ancestors saw the future so much as they were excellent guessers. That's judging from what I can do."

"How did you put it to me?" Lorna asked. "Heather can see ghosts, and they can tell her where a

buried treasure is, but you just know where the treasure is located?"

"I said dead body, not treasure." Vivien chuckled.
She smoothed the material on the ground like a picnic
blanket. "Ghosts tell Heather where the body is
buried. I just know where to look for it."

Lorna gave a small smile. "I was nice-ing it up for
you. Plus, treasure sounds romantic. Dead body sounds
like a crime scene."

"Sam's ghost led you to treasure," Sue added.

"Sam?" Kari asked.

"Long story for another day." Vivien stood over the
blanket and examined her work.

Kari followed her gaze to a white circular pattern
of symbols painted on the dark cloth. So far, so good.
She hadn't homing-pigeoned back to Creepy House.
Though she couldn't say hanging out in the theater
about to hold a conversation with the afterlife was less
unsettling.

Vivien returned to the bag as Lorna began pulling
out supplies to hand them to her. "Answering your
original question, Kari, I can accept spirits and magic
because I've always been different. For you, though,
once the shock wears off, I think you'll come to realize
that when it comes to ghosts, nothing has changed as
far as the day-to-day of it. They've always been there

and haven't messed with you. I don't think most of them are even aware we're here."

"It's been two years. I'm still waiting for the shock to wear off completely," Sue admitted.

Kari moved to look at the magical book. It looked like one of the oversized specimens kept under glass in big libraries to keep people from touching. Symbols created a circular pattern embossed on the cover to match the one on the blanket. Her hand began to vibrate, and she looked at the ring. The delicate design etched along the band matched one of the patterns on the old book and blanket.

None of this made sense. How did Julia's ring get into Connie's storage room? It's not like someone would know she'd see the home movie and be the one to find it. But then, Kari was trying to apply logic to the supernatural.

Vivien put four unlit blue candles along the sides of the blanket. Lorna followed her, dripping something from a vial onto them. Seeing her watching, Lorna said, "Basil oil for protection."

"Why do we need protection from Julia?" Kari took an involuntary step back from their makeshift altar.

"We don't." Heather joined them. "It's just a safety precaution to keep other things from slipping through."

"Like..." She glanced at Lorna. "Glenn-demons?"

"Demons, angry spirits..." Vivien gave a short laugh before finishing, "Miffed Muffys."

"The blue candles amplify our call like good cell service to the other side. The circle on the cloth will lock them inside, kind of like a ghost cage," Heather said. "If we suspect the ghost that we're about to summon is a real bastard, we'll eat blueberries. They help against psychic attacks."

"And they're full of health benefits," Lorna added. "Oh, crap! I forgot to bring pillows to sit on."

"Don't worry about it." Heather went to sit cross-legged next to a candle. "It's just Julia. We won't be on the floor long."

Sue took her place by another candle and waited.

Vivien knelt on the cloth and reached for the book. She flipped open the front cover and took out a scrap of paper. Handing it to Kari, she said, "You'll say this with us."

Lorna sat across from Heather and gave a small moan as she settled on the hard floor. "I prefer the pillows."

Vivien sat back and motioned for Kari to join them.

"But there are only four sides," she said, trying to get out of it.

"We'll make room," Vivien said. She and Heather

scooched over.

Kari reluctantly joined them. She wanted answers, but this seemed like a terrifying way to get them.

The ladies joined hands. Vivien and Heather offered their hands to Kari. Her fingers shook as she set the paper on the floor in front of her.

"Don't let go until we tell you." Heather clasped her fingers. Electricity hummed through her at the contact.

Vivien took her other hand. The candle flames lit of their own accord. Kari gasped and tried to pull away, but both Vivien and Heather tightened their hold.

As the circle completed, her hair lifted from her shoulders. Her scalp tingled. She noticed the others suffered the same effect as if a static charge flowed through the group. The overhead stage lights flickered before dimming.

Kari felt a rush of emotions flooding her. When she glanced at Heather, she felt determination, which was strange since Kari wasn't determined to do this. She was frightened.

Looking at Sue, Kari sensed fear and excitement. When she studied Lorna, she felt concern. From Vivien, she detected a sense that this was all an incredible thrill.

Kari realized these were not her feelings. The other

women's emotions were clouding hers until she didn't know *what* she should feel. Her heart beat faster, and she took a deep breath in a weak attempt to calm down.

"I know you're scared, but focus on seeing Julia," Vivien stated.

In unison, the women said, "Spirits tethered to this plane, we humbly seek your guidance."

Kari looked at the paper and tried to speak. Her mouth opened, but no sound came out as she couldn't read the words through her blurry vision.

"Spirits, search amongst your numbers for the spirit we seek," they continued. "We call forth Julia Warrick..."

Kari managed to join them finally, uttering, "from the great beyond."

Nothing happened. Kari stared at the blanket and then the chairs. She heard the panting of her breath.

"Grandma, come on," Heather said, looking around as if she couldn't see her either. "You know we're here."

"Try again," Vivien said.

This time Kari joined them, glancing up from the paper to the circle as she spoke. "Spirits tethered to this plane, we humbly seek your guidance. Spirits, search amongst your numbers for the spirit we seek. We call forth Julia War—"

"Hold your horses. I'm coming. I'm coming," a disembodied voice interrupted.

Kari held very still, too afraid to even breathe. The other women's emotions ran through her, obscuring her own.

"Julia?" Vivien asked.

"There's something repelling about the air tonight," Julia answered.

"Grandma, we want you to meet someone," Heather stated. She glanced at Vivien. "I don't know why she does this. She's the one who sent the rings out into the world for people to find. Then when they do, and we come to her for help, she acts all coy."

Kari's lungs burned, and she had to gasp for air. The loud intake projected over the stage.

A figure appeared next to Lorna, not flickering like Lori, but a still, translucent form. Julia's arm draped over Lorna's shoulder, and her head dipped forward to rest on her arm. A scarf covered her hair, and she wore a shapeless nightgown with slippers. Sadness flooded their connection as if Julia's emotions joined theirs.

No. Not sadness. Sickness.

"Julia?" Lorna released her friends' hands and gently moved to touch the ghost's shoulder. She let her fingers hover along Julia's arm.

Heather and Vivien let go of her hands. The flow of emotions stopped.

Kari couldn't take her eyes from Julia's form. The colors of her nightgown appeared faded as the black stage showed through her. The ghost lifted her head. She looked like a young woman, not someone's grandmother.

"Did she die young?" Kari whispered.

"No." Vivien shook her head. "I've never seen her like this."

Julia tugged at the scarf on her head. The material slipped off her bobbed hair only to be dropped onto the floor. It disappeared as it touched the ground.

Dark circles marred the skin beneath Julia's eyes. Her taut features looked an unnatural color. But, being as she was dead, maybe that was normal for ghosts. It's not like she had blood to rose her cheeks or life to fill her vacant eyes.

None of the ladies moved as they stared at Julia.

"Did she look like this when you were talking to her earlier?"

"No. She was in her bootlegger pant suit." Heather crossed over the blanket, ignoring the symbols on the floor. She lifted her hand toward Julia. "Grandma? Julia? What's happened?"

"I shouldn't have drunk that..." Julia's body moved as if she took a deep breath.

"Are you..." Vivien joined Heather by the ghost. Her voice carried a small laugh as she finished, "Hungover?"

Julia muttered, the words indecipherable. She indeed appeared as if she might throw up on the stage.

"Grandma, can you appear from a different time? We want to introduce you to Kari," Heather said. "She found—"

Julia screeched, half scream, half wild cry, and all a hollow echo. The noise caused the others to jump back in fright. Kari followed their lead, stumbling and ready to run. If there were ever a time that the house should make her disappear and call her back to it, now would be it.

Of course, it didn't. That would be too easy.

The horrible cry faded but left fear in its wake.

"What is she doing here?" Julia demanded, her attention focused on Kari.

"Grandma, this is Kari. She found your ring," Heather said.

"Show her," Lorna prompted, lifting her own ring finger.

Kari quickly lifted her hand to show the gold band. "My mother—"

"That's not mine," Julia yelled, her eyes accusing. "She has death on her hands. Get her out. Get her out. Get her—"

Julia burst into specks of light and disappeared. The lights flickered and came back on.

Kari stood, shaking. A tear slipped over her cheek. She slapped more than swiped it away.

The way Julia looked at her chilled her to the bone. The spirit saw what no one else could.

"She has death on her hands."

Kari hadn't realized how desperately she had hoped Julia would tell her the answers she sought— about her mother, her father, her supposed daughter. About Connie and the notebook that they had found in a box hidden in bricks.

"She has death on her hands."

Did that mean she had smothered Connie with the pillow? Murder?

Surely, she would remember doing something like that.

"What was that?" Sue asked, the words so soft Kari barely heard them. "She's never been like that."

"Heather?" Vivien turned in circles on the stage, searching.

"She's gone. I don't feel her. I..." Heather looked at Kari. Her expression was impossible to read, but Kari imagined she saw an accusation in the woman's eyes. "I don't understand."

"I didn't..." Kari shook her head in denial, slapping away another tear. "I couldn't have..."

"Julia's mistaken," Lorna said as if coming to Kari's defense. "She found a ring. The symbol on it matches one on the book. Strange things have been happening. We've seen them."

Kari grabbed the ring and pried it from her finger, ignoring the discomfort as she forced it off. She threw it on the blanket full of symbols and rushed toward the stairs. "I don't want it. I didn't ask for any of this. I'm done. Thank you for trying to help me, but—"

Kari's hand tingled, and she automatically glanced down to see the ring was back on her finger. She stopped on the stairs. She wanted to scream. And cry. And run.

She especially wanted to run.

"I didn't want any of this," she whispered.

Vivien sat on the edge of the stage and slid off the side to land in front of the seats. "Wait. Don't run."

"We all have moments when we want to hide, but you can't. Not from this," Heather said, following Vivien over the side of the stage to stand next to her. "You have more than just yourself to think about."

"She has death on her hands."

Kari looked at her hands.

"What is it?" Vivien's voice was soft.

"I have death on my hands," Kari whispered. The secret and the fear it caused was too much. It hung like an albatross around her neck. She could no longer ignore it. Maybe this all happened because she was guilty, and Connie tormented her with film projections of her mother to elicit a confession.

"I don't know what she meant by—" Heather began.

"I think I killed Connie," Kari blurted, unable to look them in the eye. She didn't want to see their judgments or their rejections. She just wanted all of this to be over.

"You think?" Heather asked.

"Maybe?" Kari closed her eyes and tried to remember. The memory of the pillow was so vivid she could feel it in her hands. "Connie was in one of her moods and was going on about some very mean things. It's no excuse, but I'd been drinking. I just remember feeling extremely cold and furious, and I..." She took a deep breath. "But you said Julia knows things, and she said I have death on my hands. I need to go to the police station. I'm turning myself in."

No one answered her.

For a moment, she worried she was back at the

house. Kari opened her eyes to find she was still in the theater. Only, instead of on the steps, she stood back onstage.

"How did you do that?" Lorna asked.

"What?" Kari looked around, out of sorts.

"You teleported from there," Vivien pointed at the stairs before moving her finger to where Kari stood now, "to there."

"You're a traveler," Lorna said with a soft smile. "That's your superpower."

"I think you mean runner," Kari admitted. "I usually run from, not travel toward."

Why were they talking about this? Didn't they hear her confess to murder?

"It makes sense." Vivien nodded. She leaned her arms on the stage floor as she stood in front of it. "Your magic is bringing you where you need to be, not where you want to go. You said the last place you wanted to be was in Connie's house, but you needed to be there to see your mother. You wanted to leave, but your magic kept you here in the theater."

"I killed Connie," Kari looked at each of them in turn. "Is no one concerned about that? I might be a murderer."

Lorna and Sue shared a look.

Heather slowly shook her head in denial.

"No," Vivien stated. "You're not a killer. I don't sense that kind of darkness about you."

"Most likely, if you did do something, something or someone possessed you." Heather walked to the stairs and came back on the stage. "You said you felt cold and sudden rage?"

Vivien nodded. "Textbook angry possession—well, if there was an actual textbook for these things."

"That ring should protect you from it happening again," Heather said. "It's a good thing your mother was so insistent you have it."

"But..." Kari looked at her hands. She'd been gripping the pillow. It was her body. "I didn't see anyone else with me. No ghosts. I was holding the pillow, and I was angry. Connie said some pretty horrible things, and I..."

Heather stopped next to her. "Do you remember doing it?"

Kari shook her head in denial.

"Then you don't know what happened," Heather concluded.

"I think it's time we talked to Connie," Lorna said. "If Julia isn't going to help us, then we need to go to the source."

"I—" Kari stiffened as light flashed.

CHAPTER TWELVE

"—DON'T KNOW IF—"

"Whoa, how'd you do that?"

Kari found herself standing in the living room of Connie's house beneath the repaired ceiling. She turned to find Angel in the doorway, staring at her. He slowly set a five-gallon bucket of white ceiling paint on the ground.

"Seriously, that was..." Angel kept his gaze on her.

"Weird?" she offered, expecting him to hightail it out of the house.

"Awesome," he finished with a surprised laugh. "Is it wrong to ask if you can do it again?"

"I can't control it," Kari said. The second they mentioned summoning Connie, she'd wanted to refuse. Vivien had been right. She teleported to the last place she wanted to go. "I understand if you want to cancel our date. I can't risk being in public right now."

"Why would I want to cancel?" Angel asked. "I got a pretty woman to say yes to me. I've already told my mother. She's ecstatic that I'm bringing a girl home, finally, and wanted to know how you felt about June weddings."

Kari's mouth opened, and she tried to think of a polite response.

"I'm joking." Angel laughed. "Not about you being a pretty woman, but about telling my mother."

Kari gave a stunned laugh as she caught on to the joke. "Funny."

"I try." He grinned. "You looked like you could use a laugh."

Damn, the man had a handsome smile. It caught her attention, and she found herself staring at his mouth. Angel touched his lip. The simple gesture distracted her focus.

"With so much chaos in my life, I haven't had a chance to say thank you for everything you've done for me." She moved closer to where he stood. "You helped put out the fire. You fixed the ceiling. You've gone above and beyond what any contractor would do under the circumstances."

For some reason, being closer to him made her

nervous. She was a grown-ass woman, and yet her heart fluttered around her chest like a teenager.

"Some guys bring flowers. I bring paint." He nodded toward the bucket.

"Can I write you a check for the work you've done?" Kari started to move past him, trying to remember where she'd left her checkbook. "I know you have workers to pay and—"

Angel touched her arm. "That's not necessary, but you could offer me a cup of coffee."

"Oh?" A tiny shiver of awareness worked over her at the contact. "Yeah. Yes. I can do that."

Kari led the way down the hall into the kitchen. The room was as sadly neglected as the rest of the house. "If you're hungry, I have every casserole combination known to man. I can put one in the oven."

"Just the coffee would be great. I planned on getting the first coat on the ceiling this evening," Angel answered. He leaned against the counter. His gaze wandered around the kitchen, seeming to trace the edge where the ceiling met the wall. "If you ever decide to renovate this place, I hope you'll let me put in a bid."

"If I do, the job is yours." She pulled a bag of coffee and filter from the cabinet. "You've more than earned it, but I don't know. I never saw myself owning a house that didn't move." Kari glanced out the window to her RV and shook her head. "Seeing the same view every morning? I don't know. It feels..."

"Boring?" he suggested

"Sedentary," she answered. "Stagnant."

However, standing in the kitchen with Angel, for the first time in a long time she didn't feel like running. He had a calming presence, and the moment felt incredibly normal—or at least what she imagined normal might be for most people.

Kari held the empty coffee pot in her hand, staring at it. She thought about being a child, watching a housekeeper make coffee in the morning. They'd always lived in beautiful homes, pristine white kitchens, and the latest trendy colors on the walls. This house would have never met Connie's standards, yet this is where her grandmother had chosen to live her final days. Had Connie felt some kind of connection to this place, the old family property? It seemed odd to think of her grandmother as nostalgic.

"Would you like me to finish?" Angel offered, gesturing at the empty pot.

"Kids need a home," Kari said. "Not RVs and campgrounds."

"Kids need love. A sense of belonging. Home is where you make it. I like to think most parents do their best. I would imagine traveling the country in an RV and meeting all kinds of different people would have life value. Are you expecting?" Angel glanced at her waist.

Kari touched her stomach. "No. I, uh, have a six-year-old."

"She with her father?"

"I don't..." Kari frowned. She looked at the empty coffee pot, trying to remember what she'd been doing with it. She couldn't focus. "I don't know. Probably not."

Angel appeared confused. He took the coffee pot from her and carried it to the sink to fill it with water. "Was there an adoption?"

"I don't..." Kari watched him fill the pot and then pour the water into the back of the coffee maker before turning it on. "It's complicated."

"Kari, what's going on? You can talk to me if you want." Angel put a hand on her shoulder. "I know you've been going through a lot with the funeral and the house." He glanced upward. "And other things."

She, too, looked at the ceiling and thought of her mother. "You're not scared of being here? With the haunting, I mean."

"The way William and Heather explained it, ghosts are everywhere. Normally people go their whole lives without realizing it. William said he spent most of his ignoring them. I wasn't scared before, so I figure I shouldn't be scared now. Though, I'll admit to being a little more curious every time I hear a strange creak in an old house."

She stared into his eyes, feeling the kindness radiating from him. "What about possessions?"

"I'm not sure what any ghost would want with me unless they miss drywall dust," Angel said. "That sounds more horror movie than real life."

Kari fisted her hands, able to feel the memory of the pillow. Horror movie was a fitting description.

"Why don't you tell me about your kid?" he prompted.

"Constance," Kari said. "That's her name."

And really, that and her age was all she knew about the girl—six-year-old Constance, named for her conniving great-grandmother.

"One second." Kari went to the dining room and found the letter from Connie. When she returned to the kitchen, she gripped it in her hands. "I had an emergency appendectomy. While I was in surgery, Connie paid a fertility doctor to harvest my eggs. She then found a surrogate and..."

Angel listened patiently, not seeming to judge one way or the other.

"I sound like the guest star of one of those bad nineties talk shows." Kari leaned her head back and sighed. The coffee pot gurgled as it started to brew. "Feel free to run at any time."

"She found a surrogate and..." He prompted.

"Here." She handed him the letter. "It's such an unbelievable story. I feel like I should just show you proof."

"You have nothing to prove to me." Angel took the letter and unfolded it.

"It's insanity. I can't even do it justice trying to explain. Connie didn't want the family line to die with me. Apparently, our bloodline is so precious the world couldn't possibly do without it." She gestured at the letter. "Go ahead. I hate secrets, they're so much work, and if you're interested in dating me, you might as well see what you're in for."

While he read, Kari watched the coffee pot for a few seconds before realizing she needed to grab mugs out of the cupboard.

"I don't have to tell you how messed up this sounds," Angel said when he'd finished reading. He refolded the paper. "How do you feel about it?"

"I guess like when a guy finds out he's a father to a first-grader." Kari set the mugs down on the counter.

"Shocked.   Confused.   Betrayed.   Worried. Unprepared."

"If I found out I had a kid that I never knew about, that'd be one thing. I mean, people have sex, and we know the risk involved. But if someone took my sperm against my will, without my knowledge, then made a life with it..." Angel shook his head and handed her the letter. "This is a whole new level of wrong. I'm sorry it happened to you."

"I'm so angry at Connie. I don't know where to focus that anger. It's insanity." Kari thought of the pillow in her hands. She couldn't tell him that part. Maybe—*hopefully*—it had been a possession. Maybe not. "But I feel sorry for the kid, you know? None of this is her fault."

Angel reached for the coffee pot and stopped it mid-brew to fill the mugs. "I have a sledgehammer you can take to the wall if it will make you feel better. Repairing it after would give me an excuse to hang around here longer."

Kari couldn't help a small laugh. She shoved the letter in her back pocket and then took the mug he offered. "You know, it might be fun, but with my luck, the roof would probably cave in on me."

"Have you tried contacting Constance?" Angel asked.

Kari shook her head. "I tried to find an address in the packet the lawyer gave me, but there was nothing. I guess I have to start driving around to all the properties I inherited to try to find her, but I can't drive because, well, you saw how I appeared out of thin air. I can't control when it happens. Maybe it's for the best she's not here. This place isn't exactly child friendly at the moment."

"Have you thought about hiring a private investigator?" Angel asked. "I have a cousin. He's a little obnoxious but discreet. He mostly hunts down guys who skip out on their bonds."

"I don't know. Maybe."

"Or what about this doctor?" Angel motioned toward where the letter was in her pocket. "The one who has more of your..."

"Eggs?" Kari supplied.

"I'm not sure what the first-date etiquette is on discussing a woman's eggs." Angel set his coffee down without taking a drink. Steam rose from inside the mug.

"Date?" Kari felt that tiny thrill rush through her again.

"I'm nothing if not a hopeful opportunist," he teased.

"Or a glutton for punishment," Kari countered. "How are you not running away right now?"

Angel moved closer. "Because I like you, Kari Grove. There's something special about you. I noticed it the first time I saw you walking down the stairs. I was sure you would see how nervous I was but after everything that happened..."

Kari remembered thinking how handsome he was and how much Connie would hate it if she dated a blue-collar man.

She needed Connie out of her head. Who cared what her grandmother would have thought about Angel? He had shown her great kindness and had an openness that sometimes felt rare in the world.

"I'm not happy Heather and William's mom needed emergency surgery, but I am glad you were the one to answer the call to help me." Kari felt the heat radiating from him as he gravitated closer.

Angel lifted his hand, letting it hover close to her cheek without touching her. "Would I be out of line if I kissed you?"

She shook her head. "I can't guarantee that nothing weird will happen if you do."

The handsome grin spread over his mouth. "I'm willing to risk it."

His fingers brushed her cheek, and he leaned

slowly into her. The first brush of his mouth caused a tiny shiver to roll through her at the intimate contact. She glanced around the kitchen, unable to help but wonder if some invisible being watched them.

"Did you change your mind?" he asked, pulling back.

"Just wondering if we're about to put on a supernatural peep show." Kari chuckled.

Angel continued to smile as he leaned in to kiss her again, this time deeper.

All the fear and emotions she'd been feeling since coming to Freewild Cove churned inside her, needing to come out. Kari grabbed hold of his shoulders and returned the kiss. He moaned softly, and she leaned fully into him. His hands journeyed down her back to her hips.

Kari turned with him to lean against the kitchen counter.

She'd fantasized about moments like this, alone, in her RV, boondocked out in some isolated field. Life on the road didn't give much opportunity for sexual relationships, and she'd never been a pick-up-a-guy-in-a-bar type of gal. But now that it was happening, none of the nervous insecurities she thought she'd feel came into play. With Angel, she felt safe.

Earlier, she had compared the fluttering in her

stomach to being a teenager. She'd been wrong. When they kissed, she felt like a grown-ass woman—none of the inept insecurities of her teens and twenties or the body-aging insecurities of her thirties.

Hands began to explore as the kiss became more passionate. She pulled on his shirt, lifting it in a subtle invitation as her fingers found flesh.

Angel pulled back. "Are you sure?"

Kari nodded.

He glanced up. "Should we go...?"

"Here's good," she said, pulling his face back to hers to resume kissing.

She explored the length of his back, finding a long, thin scar surrounded by smooth skin. The gentle rise and fall of his breath caused his muscles to move beneath her hands. Her heart beat faster as desire flooded all reason.

Angel lifted her onto the counter to bring her mouth more in line with his. Strong hands gripped her thighs. He took his time as if each stroke asked her permission to continue.

"Kari?" Lorna's yell came from the front door, and it felt like someone chucked an ice cube at their heads. "Are you here? We came as fast as we—"

Kari pulled back from the kiss, but before she could answer, a light flashed. Her legs dropped down straight. When she could again focus her vision, she realized she'd transported them out of the kitchen into the small bedroom of her RV. With the sliders pulled in, the walls of the room pressed up against the bed to leave only a narrow hallway to maneuver through.

"That was..." Angel still held onto her. He glanced around the tight space. The blinds were closed and the dim light peeking through from outside hid more than it revealed. "Did you teleport us?"

"You came with me," she answered in surprise. "No one has ever traveled with me."

Of course, it was the first time she'd been touching someone when it happened.

"That was a neat trick." He gave a small laugh as he faced her. No part of him seemed frightened by what had happened. "It tickled."

Vivien had mentioned she appeared to teleport to where she needed to be. Apparently, her newfound magic believed she needed to be alone with Angel.

Good magic.

His eyes glanced over her face before concentrating on her mouth.

Kari grinned. "Where were we?"

She pulled him so that he fell onto the bed with her, and the new position allowed for more unrestricted movement. He took off his shirt before slowly peeling away her clothes. His calloused hands contrasted with the gentle warmth of his caresses. The press of his arousal settled near her thigh, blocked by the stiff material of his pants.

Kari reached for the nightstand and pulled out an old box of condoms. Just because she didn't have sex often didn't mean she didn't travel prepared. She dropped it next to them on the bed.

The intensity of their passion built. She didn't want this to stop. The pleasure helped erase the pain and made her forget the world of trouble hanging over her.

The dark room created a game of exploration as it suppressed one sense, only to enhance others. She felt him smile against her. Hands cupped her naked breasts. The smell of his skin, of soap and cologne, filled her nose. She heard the sound of his breathing mingling with her soft moans and gasps for air. The taste of his kiss lingered on her mouth. Everything about him was new and enticing.

Angel took his time exploring her body. When he finally shifted his hips to come over her, Kari handed him the box of condoms. She listened as he opened it and pulled a pillow under her head.

Angel settled between her legs. She shivered at the intimate brush of their bodies coming together. He made love to her slowly, as if he had nowhere else to be. When she met her release, he pressed his cheek against hers. Kari gripped his shoulders as he joined her in shared climax. Warm, shuddering breaths fanned her neck.

Angel rolled next to her on the bed and gathered her into his arms. She wished there was more light so she could see his face.

"Kari?" Heather called as a knock sounded on the RV's cabin door. "Are you in there?"

"The lights aren't on," Vivien said. "I don't hear anything."

"Where else do you think she transported to?" Heather asked. "I'm starting to worry."

A phone began to ring.

"Should—?" Angel whispered.

"It's unlocked," Vivien said to the sound of the door opening. "I think I sense someone inside."

Kari opened her mouth to answer her new friends. Light flashed, and they were transported into the guest room inside Connie's house.

Kari sat up on the bed in surprise. Light streamed into the windows brighter than the RV bedroom, just like she'd wanted. She turned to Angel, who was naked beside her. He was slower to push up.

"I don't know why I keep doing that," Kari said, studying his face.

He smiled and cupped her cheek. "I'm just glad you keep bringing me with you. How many guys can say they teleport during sex?"

Kari couldn't help but laugh with him. "I still don't know how you're not freaking out right now. Honestly, your calm about it is probably the only thing keeping *me* calm."

"Is it strange? Sure." He leaned to the side to force her eyes to meet his. "Is strange worth it? Definitely, if it means I get to spend time with you. I don't know if you realize this, Kari, but you have me completely enamored."

"I like you, too," she answered.

He gave her a quick kiss before pulling back. "You should probably let them know you're all right. They sounded concerned."

Kari nodded. She didn't want to leave him. "You're right. I'll go now. We were supposed to summon Connie's ghost before I disappeared on them."

"That must be difficult," Angel said. "When they séanced my aunt Mariana to speak to my mom, I could see how hard it was on her. She wanted to hug her sister so badly. I have to admit it was strange for me too. Mariana was there, but not there."

Kari nodded to acknowledge what he said. "I think this séance is going to be a little different."

She couldn't bring herself to tell him what she might have done. Her attention turned to the wall that separated them from Connie's room. She half-expected Connie to walk through the wall to express her disappointment. Kari naturally leaned closer to Angel.

"Hey, it'll be all right." He hugged her to his chest. "The ladies have a way of doing things. You'll be protected."

She wished that were true.

"We didn't hug in my family," Kari said. "There is a big part of me that hopes Connie has moved on and a séance doesn't work."

"Think of it as closure."

"You're right. I need to let them know I'm here." She started to stand and realized she was naked. "Oh, crap."

"What?"

Kari searched the bed. "I didn't transport your clothes with us. I don't have anything that will fit you."

At that, Angel laughed and stood up from the bed. He grabbed a blanket and wrapped it around his waist like a toga. "No worries. I'll go get them."

Kari made a move to stop him. "Wait."

His pleasant demeanor faded some. "Embarrassed to be seen with me?"

"No, of course not." Kari crossed the room naked to stand by him. "I just wanted to say I had fun, and I'm not ready for it to be over. I hope we can have a coffee date again sometime soon."

"You can bet on it." Angel grinned and pulled her close. "In fact, I insist."

CHAPTER THIRTEEN

"I HAVE SO MANY INAPPROPRIATE QUESTIONS," Vivien said as Kari came down the stairs.

Angel had gone down minutes before her, and it was no surprise Vivien would be the one to catch him. Thankfully, Kari had clothes in the guest room and didn't have to wear a blanket toga like some kind of dorm room walk of shame—not that any part of her felt shame in what she'd done with Angel. Though, she hadn't had another pair of shoes in the room and was currently barefoot.

Kari paused on the steps and gave a sheepish grin. She buried her hands in her hair as she stretched. "The answer to all of them will be yes."

Vivien laughed. "Glad to hear it. I'm assuming

Angel is going for his clothes in the RV. We saw them next to the bed."

"I'm sorry if my disappearance worried all of you. I seem to be teleporting around this place quite a bit." Kari came all the way down the stairs and glanced around but only found Vivien. "I know we were talking about contacting Connie. I didn't expect to be sidetracked. Things just sort of happened."

"You never have to apologize to me about that." Vivien grinned. "Life is for living. Besides, you appear more relaxed."

"I am." Kari took a deep breath. However, the idea of contacting Connie caused the weight to return to her shoulders.

"We were discussing it and thought maybe it would be good to take a break from séancing tonight. Sue is helping her boyfriend with inventory. She offered to cancel, but we kind of have a rule that life needs to keep moving even when the supernatural comes out to play. I promised to call her if we needed her." Vivien pointed toward the kitchen. "Lorna is cooking if you can count reheating casseroles as cooking."

"I count reheating a drive-thru burrito in the microwave as cooking, so I vote yes," Kari said. She heard sounds coming from the kitchen.

Vivien lifted her hands as if to feel Kari's aura and nodded in approval. "You really do seem to be in a better place. That's good. I think it might help you get through this to have your anxiety levels down. The energy coming off you has definitely calmed."

Kari took a deep breath and let it out slowly. The knot in her stomach had lessened. "I do feel better."

Vivien dropped her hands. "Anyway, since you magically hightailed it out of the theater when we mentioned summoning you-know-who, we thought maybe you would need a break while we regrouped, so to speak."

"Where's Heather?" Kari remembered hearing her outside the RV.

"She got a call from her high school contact." Vivien moved toward the dining room. "She went to pick up the old yearbooks."

"Smells great," Angel said from the kitchen.

"I can't take credit. This one was from, uh," Lorna paused for a moment, and then it sounded like she read, "Mr. and Mrs. Fisher."

Kari waited in the hall, watching for Angel.

"I'm not sure what it is," Lorna continued, "but there is a lot of cheese involved."

"Can't miss with cheese," Angel answered as he came from the kitchen.

Kari smiled to see him. He wore his painter's clothes and looked ready to work.

"Hey." He smiled as he came for her.

"Hey," she answered.

"Hey," Vivien said with a small laugh from where she sat in the dining room.

Angel ignored Vivien as he stopped to give Kari a quick kiss. "Anything you need..."

"I know, you'll be in the living room." She kissed him again.

Kari watched until he turned into the living room. She let loose a captured breath.

Vivien slid the envelope from Kari's lawyer over the table, batting it back and forth between her hands. She smiled at Kari. "He's crazy about you. I don't need my magic to sense that much."

"I like him too," Kari said.

"I think it's a little more than *like*," Vivien chuckled, "but I'm told I mettle too much without being asked. It's something I'm working on. Since finding Julia's ring, my abilities have become stronger and are harder to control."

"I don't mind your insights." Kari joined her at the table.

Vivien studied Kari for a moment and then reached to take her hand. "You have nothing to be nervous about. Angel is as solid as they come. He's a loyal friend."

"You make him sound a little too good to be true." Kari didn't want perfection. It was an impossible standard to live up to.

"If it helps, he can't sing worth a damn." Vivien let go of her hand. "Trust me, I've heard him on the job sites. But the man does have some sweet-ass dance moves if you're into Cabbage Patch and The Running Man."

Kari laughed. "That good, huh?"

Vivien nodded. "His heart is in the right place, and that's all that matters."

"Whose heart?" Heather joined them. She carried a stack of yearbooks in her arms. "Oh, hey, I see Angel is painting the ceiling. It's looking fantastic in there."

"Angel's heart," Vivien said. "Kari wrote her name all over it."

"How very high school of you." Heather smiled in Kari's direction while her eyes remained on the books she held. "I'm happy to hear that."

"He is hanging close in case she needs him, under the guise of painting," Vivien added. "Everything I'm picking up from him is very sweet."

Kari bit her lip and tried to hide her pleasure at the statement. As unnerving as it was to know someone could read her emotions and inner thoughts, she liked hearing Vivien's insights into her budding relationship because they confirmed what she felt when she was with him.

"Did you get them all?" Kari asked Heather.

Vivien pushed aside the manila envelope to make room for the yearbooks.

Heather looked at the spines. "We have seventy-five, missing seventy-six, and have seventy-seven to eighty-two."

The sound of Angel working came from the other room, distracting her thoughts back to him. There was comfort in knowing he was close by.

"Hand me a couple of those. We'll look up Washington in the index." Vivien held out her hands toward Heather.

"I'll take nineteen-eighty to eighty-one," Kari said, "when my mom would have graduated."

Lorna appeared. "Food's cooking. Did you get the books?"

"Here," Heather handed her a yearbook. "We're looking for Washington."

Kari tried to look up the name Washington in the index. She ran her finger down the list of names.

"No Washington," Vivien said as she searched her books.

"Me neither," Heather said.

"Nope," Lorna added.

Kari didn't see her father's name in the first year-book. "Not in here."

"No Washington in this one either," Vivien said.

Kari searched the last book. Disappointment filled her as she searched the list twice. "And no Washington in this one. Dammit."

"I'm sorry." Heather took out the small notebook she carried in her front pocket and began writing. "But we won't give up. I'll make a list of surrounding high schools and start calling around. He might have been from another town."

"What if he's not?" Kari asked.

"Then we call every Washington listed in the Chicago phone book until someone knows who he was," Vivien said. "And we'll check obituaries for the day you were born."

"I tried that," Kari admitted. "When they started putting archived articles online, I searched for bus accidents. Now that I have a name, maybe I can find something."

Kari looked for Grove in the index and found several pages listed for her mother. Her hands trembled as she turned to the first listing. Lori's young face was one of thirty in a group photo for academic achievers. She looked bored.

The next was for orchestra. Lori held a violin. And she still looked bored.

The third was for the track team. And, yep, bored.

The fourth was her mother onstage dressed as a Victorian-looking woman as an extra in a play. A smile spread over Lori's face. The only extracurricular performance arts Connie would have approved of were honors choir and symphony orchestra. Under the photo, the caption read, "Lori Grove as Martha Washington."

Fwap-fwap-fwap...

Kari gasped, spinning in her seat to look behind her. She felt Vivien's hand on her shoulder and knew the others also saw the ghosts.

Lori stood in the old-fashioned theater dress with her hands on her hips.

"What are you doing in here?" her mother scolded. "Turn that off. You're going to get me in trouble."

"I'm recording history, Lady Washington," her father's voice answered. "Show me what's under that dress."

... fwap-fwap-fwap...

"What would President Washington think if he

heard you talking to me like that?" Lori laughed. She swayed her skirt playfully as she flirted.

"Just call me Mr. Washington," her father said. "Tell him you got confused."

Lori's expression fell, and she glanced behind her. In a panic, she said, "Mrs. Mender is coming. You have to get—"

...fwap...fwap.

The image disappeared.

"Mom?" Kari whispered. The ghost image did not return.

"So, not Washington," Heather stated the obvious. "That was a pet name."

"Keep looking," Vivien encouraged.

Kari was slower to find the next page on her mother's listing. It was Lori's senior class picture. She looked around, but no image appeared.

"Only one left," Kari said.

"Under the Stars," Heather read the page title when Kari turned to it. "A prom night to remember."

Kari pointed at a picture of her parents dancing wildly on the dance floor. Her father wore a tux jacket over a t-shirt, captured in some Elvis hip-twist move, while Lori in a sparkling pink eighties dress pressed her hands into the air. "That's them."

"Lori Grove gets down with date Derek Miller," Vivien read the caption.

"Derek Miller," Kari repeated. She had a name. "My father is Derek Miller."

Fwap-fwap-fwap...

"Derek, what are you doing?" Lori whispered.

Kari, Heather, Vivien, and Lorna all turned toward the sound. A hand looked as if it reached through the wall.

A loud thud came from the living room, followed by several thumps.

"Kari!" Angel yelled.

Kari shot up from her chair as they all ran toward the living room. Angel sat on the floor as if he'd fallen off his metal ladder. She reached to help him up and he pointed toward the wall dividing the living room from the dining room.

Ghost image Derek was on a spectral wooden straight ladder in his prom t-shirt, climbing toward the ceiling. The scene came from a low angle as if the camera were sitting on the floor.

...fwap-fwap-fwap...

"Are you all right?" Kari asked, reaching to help him up.

"Yeah. Fine." He stood close to her as he stared at the ghost projection.

"Derek, come on, let's just get out of here," Lori insisted. She stepped through the blurry edges of the scene into view. She wore Derek's tux jacket over her prom gown. "Jill said she thought she could score some beer."

"Tonight's perfect. She won't expect you home for hours. I want to see what that bitch is up to in her secret room," he answered. "Maybe we can blackmail her into leaving us alone."

"It doesn't matter," Lori insisted. "The second we graduate, we're out of here."

"Hand me the camera." Derek reached his hand down and grabbed at the air with his fingers.

...fwap-fwap-fwap...

Lori ran to the camera and picked it up. She blurred from the scene as Derek became more prominent in the image. "You left it on."

"I must have bumped it." Derek's hand became huge as he reached for it, the fingers blocking the lens.

Lorna took a step back as it came close to where she stood. The image shifted as if Derek had climbed the ladder with the camera facing downward. They saw his feet move higher until the image of them disappeared into the ceiling. The projection sound became softer but continued.

...fwap-fwap-fwap...

"Where's he going?" Lorna asked.

Angel put his hand on Kari's shoulder.

"Upstairs. Come on!" Heather ran out of the living room. They followed her up the stairs to the storage room.

...fwap-fwap-fwap...

They crowded inside. The sound became louder.

"Where...?" Lorna whispered.

"There," Angel pointed toward the exterior wall. It wasn't the same side Derek's image had climbed, but the one with the window. A ghostly image overlaid the window frame before slithering across the floor to show a thick orange rug as Derek angled the camera from outside to record within.

Angel again put a comforting hand on Kari's shoulder, standing close.

...fwap-fwap-fwap...

They all moved back as if unconsciously not wanting to block any of the show. Angel's hand slid down her arm to hold hers.

From the orange rug grew a low, round table with what appeared to be a cauldron on top. Dried herbs and potion bottles were set out next to it. The camera had only captured one side of the scene, and Kari moved closer to the window to see better.

They could make out the back of a figure standing

along the blurry edge. Muffled voices began to speak but were difficult to make out.

A woman in a denim dress stepped forward, looking down as if she held something in her hands. It appeared to be Connie's notebook.

"That's Connie," Kari whispered as if the ghosts might hear her and stop their play.

Connie turned toward the cauldron. Her grandmother looked much younger than when Kari knew her.

"This is going too far," a voice said, clear but still muted by the fact the camera was outside recording.

"I know that voice." Lorna leaned forward as if to see what was not there.

A woman appeared from the blurred edges into the scene to confront Connie.

"Grandma Julia," Heather said.

Kari could see the resemblance. Julia looked much older than the ghost that had yelled at her in the theater, but it was the same woman. She wore a green dress with large white flowers on it in a style similar to Connie's.

...*fwap-fwap-fwap*...

"You're meddling in things you don't understand," Julia scolded.

"I'm tired of you always acting like you have the

moral high ground," Connie snapped. "If it were your son about to ruin his life, you'd interfere. You know you would."

"They're just kids," Julia insisted. "Kids fall in and out of love all the time. Just wait it out."

"Lori is my daughter. She's destined for greatness, and some punk is not going to come and ruin everything I've been working for. If you think I married into the mealy-mouthed Grove family out of love, you're crazier than my mother-in-law." Connie shook her head. She placed her notebook on the table. "This is the only way to keep Lori safe and on the path to greatness."

"Uh, Kari?" Angel tapped her shoulder.

Kari glanced back, not wanting to turn, only to find Lori's transparent form stood with them. She jumped a little in surprise. Angel inched them away from her mother's spirit.

"Heather, look," Vivien said. "Lori's here."

Lori's head bent forward, and she wore a hospital gown. The ghost stared at Connie, not moving save the twitching of her hands. Her body didn't flicker like before. At Lori's presence, the image of Connie and Julia cleared as if it was no longer a projection. The soft *fwap-fwap* stopped.

"Death magic should not be trifled with," Julia

lectured, her voice stronger and her features becoming clearer. "No one should try to take power over life and death. There is a reason we don't mess with dark magic."

"Says the woman who talks to ghosts," Connie dismissed. "Don't be dramatic. I'm not killing anyone. This is a sixth-level severing spell, not the apocalypse."

"There is a reason we don't mess with this stuff. All the spells from that book are considered death magic," Julia argued. "They always—*always*—have unexpected consequences. If you do this—"

"You're just jealous that I know something you don't. You hate that I'm becoming more powerful than you are." Connie looked at her notebook and then her herbs. "Now, either help me like you said you would or be quiet. This has to happen during this lunar cycle. It's the only reason I let Lori go out tonight even though I know she's going to meet up with Derek at the dance after she promised me that she wouldn't."

"I didn't agree to help with this," Julia said. "You said you wanted to bless her future since she's graduating from high school. That is the only reason I agreed to come here tonight. I thought at worst you wanted to give her college acceptance letters a little nudge."

"That's exactly what I'm doing. Do you think that

little punk supports her going to college?" Connie snorted. "I'm protecting her."

"Connie." Julia grabbed the woman's arm. "If you do this, that's it. Our friendship is over. For good this time. No more séances, no spells, no—"

"Then leave already," Connie yelled. "But when you need help for your son Wayne, don't come crawling to me."

Connie lifted bundles of herbs over the cauldron and ran her fingers along the stalks to drop the dried petals inside. Suddenly frowning, she crossed to the window as if she'd heard something.

When Connie was distracted, Julia pulled a ring off her finger and lifted it to her lips. She whispered something before kissing the jewelry. She quickly placed it close to the base of the cauldron, in a shadow where it would be difficult to see it.

"Please reconsider," Julia begged as she moved toward the door.

Connie stood by the window and said nothing as she watched Julia leave. Then, scowling, she crossed back to her cauldron. Under her breath, she muttered, "I'm doing this for Lori. She doesn't know what's good for her. It's my place to protect her."

As Connie angrily put herbs in her cauldron, Kari

released Angel's hand and moved to look at the ring Julia left behind.

"Is it your ring?" Heather asked.

Kari watched to see if Connie would acknowledge her before leaning over to check. Connie continued on her rant, not seeing the intruders. Kari glanced at the delicately carved jewelry and nodded.

"Yes. It's my—" Kari looked up to see Connie staring right at her. She froze and held her breath in fear.

Suddenly the scene disappeared.

Kari turned to Lori's ghost.

Lori stared where Connie had been, her entire being shaking. Kari's hand vibrated where she wore the ring.

"That's a lot of anger," Vivien said, gesturing Lorna and Heather to back up before waving Angel to go toward the door.

"Kari." Angel reached toward her, refusing to leave.

"Mom?" Kari inched toward her mother.

This was not the happy teenager she'd seen in past projections. Lori exuded rage. Kari felt it coming off her in hot psychic waves, leaving her stomach in knots.

Dark circles lined Lori's sunken eyes in what

appeared to be bloodless translucent skin. Her hair hung limp and greasy around her face, giving the illusion that she hadn't bathed in days. Her hands twitched as if trying to build the energy to grab hold of something.

Lori stutter-stepped toward Kari, jerking and twitching at the effort it took to move. She stared so hard that Kari couldn't look away.

"Kari, we need to get out of here," Heather said. "This isn't right."

"That's not your mother's energy," Vivien added. "That thing is pissed and ready to fight."

"Kari, come this way, slowly," Lorna insisted from the doorway.

Angel appeared at Kari's side. He lifted his hands between them as if to hold Lori back as he shielded Kari with his body. Lori stopped walking and turned her attention to him.

"Run," Angel whispered.

Kari wanted to listen but couldn't move her legs. "She won't hurt me."

Kari wished she actually believed that. No one else seemed to.

"Angel, don't get in her way." Kari tried to push him aside, but he held firm. "I don't need you to protect me."

"I'm going to try anyway," he countered. "Run. I'll be right behind you."

Still, Kari couldn't move.

Lori suddenly swept out her hand.

Angel lifted off his feet and flew toward the door. Lorna screamed in surprise. He landed with a thud as he crashed against the door frame.

"Angel?" Kari yelled, trying to break free from her mother's thrall.

A cold chill worked over her, and Kari felt her mother's rage building. The others were talking to her, but their voices sounded far away. She saw Angel in her peripheral coming toward her.

Lori's mouth opened, but no sound came out. The ghost pressed forward, coming up against Kari's chest in an arctic blast of freezing-cold liquid rage.

CHAPTER FOURTEEN

Rage.

Pure, white-hot rage.

Burning, molten-lava kind of rage.

Kari's nerves exploded with fury, each synapse firing into her body to build the emotion until it translated into physical pain. She couldn't see, couldn't breathe, couldn't even move. The debilitating sensation took over everything else, locking her into place.

She wanted to reach out for human contact, but she was trapped in the dark, alone. So very, very alone. That great emptiness was endless, stretching out ahead of her like an eternity, falling behind her like centuries. In that knowledge came a new pain, worse than the anger.

She was alone.

Her heart was broken, and she was alone.

Kari screamed into the darkness, violently thrashing before she managed to open her eyes. She was on Connie's bedroom floor, behind the bed, hidden away from the door. Thick material swathed her body, keeping her immobile as it pinned her limbs to her sides. Only her head was allowed freedom, and she took it, twisting and banging her head as she tried to wriggle free.

Arms wrapped around her from behind like a vise. Kari bucked against their hold. Everything ached, from her pounding head to her tight muscles, to her stiff joints. Even her eyeballs burned, scratching uncomfortably each time she blinked. She tried to scream, but her throat was raw, and only grunts of anger made it past her throat.

"I got you. I got you," someone whispered as the hold on her tightened.

Her energy drained quickly, and she looked around in confusion. How did she get on the floor of Connie's room? She'd been in the storage room just seconds ago. Was this another teleport? Traveling had never felt like this.

"Let go of me," Kari croaked, thrashing once more for good measure before going limp.

"I got you." Angel held her from behind.

"Kari?" Heather appeared in front of her. "Are you back?"

"Back?" Kari rested against Angel's chest, feeling him breathe. She tried to figure out what was happening. "Do I have soul splinters?"

"Soul splinters?" Angel repeated. "I think she's delusional. Maybe we should get her to a doctor."

"It's something Lorna said after being magically transported through the walls of the house," Heather told him. "It's fine. I think she's coming back to us."

"Did I travel?" Kari asked, still confused.

"No, sweetie, you didn't transport through the house," Heather said, her voice soothing. "Angel, you can let her go."

Angel's hold eased, and Kari could push her arms free. Now able to move, she looked around to find the room wrecked. Bedding had been thrown off the bed. A pair of scissors protruded from the torn mattress as if someone had stabbed it multiple times. Pictures had been ripped from the walls and a dresser overturned.

"Careful of the glass," Heather warned as she came closer, sliding her shoes rather than walking. She cradled her arm against her chest.

Kari saw tiny shards spread over the floor. The multiple colors indicated they came from different objects. A distinct smell drew her attention to a dark spot wetting the wall over a smashed kerosene lamp.

Angel stood behind her and then hooked his hands under her arms to help her stand. The thick comforter fell from around her body. Kari winced in pain and lifted a bloody hand. A deep cut ran between two bruised knuckles.

"What happened?" Stunned, she looked around the destroyed bedroom. A pillow had been stabbed, and its feathers settled over some of the debris. Connie's clothes were ripped and thrown haphazardly around. A bra hung from the light fixture.

"Lorna's going to be all right," Vivien said from the door. The woman had blood on her shirt but didn't appear injured. "How's Kari?"

"Back with us," Heather answered.

Angel supported Kari by the arm and kept her from falling over. She turned to him. A bruise started to darken his cheek near his eye.

"What happened?" Kari asked again. Tears entered her eyes. She tried to flex her hand, but the knuckles had begun to swell. "Why do we look like we were in a bar fight?"

"You want the good news or bad news?" Vivien asked.

Kari stared at her. The feelings of anger and loneliness lingered.

"Okay. Good news first. We're pretty sure we know what happened to Connie, and it's not your fault," Vivien said.

Kari looked at the bed, remembering the feel of the pillow in her hands.

"If the rage fest we just witnessed is any indication, you definitely did not kill her," Vivien continued. "Well, not you-you."

"What happened?" Kari said, yet again fighting the fog over her thoughts. "Why can't I remember this?"

"You were possessed," Heather stated. "I guess we were wrong. The ring should have protected you from possession, but it didn't—at least not from Lori. Her rage is stronger than the magic of the ring."

"Lori had some unresolved mommy issues, and she used you to work through them," Vivien added. "I can't say I completely blame her for the anger after we saw Connie trying to hex her with dark magic. That's bad enough, but it makes me wonder what all we didn't see between them."

"My mother...?" Kari shook her head, not wanting to believe it. All that anger and pain came from Lori? "She did all this?"

"Afraid so," Heather answered. "Though, in my opinion, Connie did more than *try* to hex her. I remember Grandma Julia warning us against playing around with spells, especially with what she called death magic—killing things, killing people, killing love, killing business deals, all of it. She said it was negative magic, and it always came with consequences. You never get something for nothing. It sounded like Connie cast a severing spell to tear your parents apart, and it ended badly."

"Angel?" Kari touched his cheek lightly. "I'm so sorry. Did I do that to your face?"

"It's fine. Doesn't hurt. Lori did it when I tried to restrain her," he answered. "I don't think she was aiming to hurt me, per se. I was just in the way. She did have a few choice things to say about your grandmother."

"That brings us to the bad news," Vivien said.

Kari looked at her expectantly.

Vivien didn't meet her gaze. "I don't want to tell her."

"Angel's right. Lori did have a lot to say or *scream*. Connie's meddling was responsible for her death." Heather frowned at Vivien. "You're the one who felt what was happening. You need to tell her."

"Your mom has been harboring rage for a long time." Vivien rubbed her arms. "I don't think the Lori that did this was your mother, not anymore. Those bricks we found, the brick dust that people used to draw barriers, it's all used to keep ghosts out."

"Or trapped in, depending on the intent," Heather inserted. "The room was so dirty it was difficult to see a difference in dust, but I'm guessing Connie had drawn a line of brick dust around the open end of the box fort by the projector to cage Lori."

"Why?" Kari asked.

"Connie had Lori trapped in the storage room since shortly after her death," Vivien answered. "And I think that is why her spirit is tortured."

Kari frowned. "Why would she do that? What possible purpose would it serve?"

"From the images and feelings I got off your mom, I've deduced Lori came back to the place where Connie first cast the spell, to her childhood home," Vivien answered. "When Connie realized she had an angry daughter haunting this house, she used the projector and old films you found to lure her into the storage room and then brick-boxed her in to keep her in line. She then locked up the house and left her here. Lori has been festering in anger, alone, in the dark for forty years, with nothing but recorded memories to remind her of who she was and what she'd lost. That's enough to tarnish even the best of souls. I'll bet she was waiting for a chance to escape."

"I don't think Lori is really Lori anymore, at least not as she had been in life," Heather added. "She's more like a vengeful spirit now. They don't make logical decisions but are merely a reflection of rage and bitter disappointments."

"The weight of bricks took their toll on the ceiling. Cracked it." Angel didn't sound as confident in his assessment as the others.

"It could have been enough for her to slip out of her prison, especially when her long-lost baby showed up on the other side of the crack," Heather said. "Your strong emotion toward what Connie said to you probably opened the door to the possession. In no way should you hold yourself responsible."

"That's why this place looks like it hasn't been decorated since the seventies." Kari had often wondered about the dated décor. She poked a bare toe at broken shards of glass. She'd not put shoes on after she and Angel had made love. "I always thought it was strange. Connie had been meticulous about her homes."

"William told me once that renovations can stir hauntings." Angel coughed and cleared his throat. "Excuse me. Dust."

"I find it a lot stranger that Connie chose to come here to die rather than stay away to keep her dirty little secret. She had to have known someone would open the storage room and that Lori's ghost would get out," Lorna said.

"Maybe that is what she wanted," Vivien mused.

"Let's get you out of this room," Angel stated.

Kari looked at him in surprise as he swept her up into his arms to carry her. She would have protested, but she felt too weak to walk much on her own and trying to make her way over broken glass in bare feet didn't sound like a good plan. His boots crunched over the glass as he carried her out of the bedroom.

Vivien and Heather stepped out of his way. He walked her toward the stairs and held her for a moment as if he contemplated carrying her down.

"Here's good," Kari said, stopping him. "Thank you."

He nodded and reluctantly placed her on the floor.

Instead of going down, Kari walked toward the storage room. The door frame was cracked from where Angel had been thrown into the wood. She touched it lightly and glanced at him.

"I'm okay," he softly assured her.

She stared into the empty room where the projector had been. Forty years confined to a small space, with only box walls and film reels to keep her company, sounded like a nightmare.

Kari remembered the feelings she'd had during the possession. Not *like* a nightmare. It *was* a nightmare.

"This explains why Lori wanted you to see her past. She was showing you the only way she could, through the recorded images of her memories." Vivien pushed a curl behind Kari's ear in a loving gesture. "I don't think Lori meant the fire to hurt you as much as it was a projection of her loss. Seeing you watching her on-screen must have triggered her."

"If it were me, I'd want to burn them too, so they could never be used to trap me again." Kari looked at the walls, remembering all the items shoved into the room—plastic bins, mannequins, and sheet-covered furniture. Hell, there had even been a creepy pile of ratty, broken dolls. And the windows had been covered to keep out the sunlight. "She was packed away in here like some forgotten family heirloom."

"Heather, do you see her?" Vivien asked.

Heather shook her head in denial. "I doubt she'll be back for a while, not after that tirade."

Heather's phone rang, and she pulled it from her back pocket. She held up her finger to indicate she needed a moment and disappeared down the hallway. Kari heard her feet going down the stairs.

"Where's Lorna?" Kari asked. "You said she was going to be all right. Was she hurt?"

"She was in the way when Lori tried to leave." Vivien motioned toward the stairs. "She's downstairs resting on the couch. Sue is on her way. We weren't sure if we were going to have to serve some kind of eviction notice on your mom, but she burned herself out fairly quickly and left on her own."

It hadn't felt quick. It had felt like forever.

"It's just as well," Vivien continued. "Instead, we'll work on getting Lori and Connie to talk to each other. That show should be worth the price of admission."

"Angel, if you want to go, I won't blame you," Kari said. "I think it's time we tried to get some straight answers out of Connie and Lori. You might not want to stick around for round two."

"I'm not leaving you," Angel quickly denied the offer. "I'll stand outside if you kick me out, but I'm not leaving you."

"Good," Vivien inserted. "We're going to need all the energy we can get. Angel, be a dear and find Kari something with a lot of sugar in it, please. She looks like she's about to pass out."

Angel seemed relieved to have an assignment that let him stay inside the house and went to do as Vivien requested.

When they were alone, Kari frowned. "Maybe I should make him go. It isn't safe in here."

"Are you kidding?" Vivien chuckled. "All that virile, protective male energy is exactly what we need. Something has got to fuel these ghosts. Besides, it would be meaner to make that poor guy leave. He'd chew off his own hand to protect you."

Kari couldn't help her smile.

"You haven't felt it yet, have you?" Vivien asked.

"What? Love?" Kari laughed.

"Relief," Vivien corrected. "You didn't hurt Connie. It wasn't you."

Kari's expression fell. Vivien was right. She looked at her hands, curling her fingers as if she held the pillow. It hadn't been her fault.

"Ah, there it is," Vivien whispered. "Relief. Good. You won't have that burden clouding you when we start the séance. Hopefully, things will go a little better this time around."

CHAPTER FIFTEEN

KARI STOOD in the storage room, staring at the blue cloth lying in the middle of the floor. The edge covered the plywood repair over where she'd fallen through. Vivien had placed Julia's séance book in the middle before setting candles around the edges, pausing to anoint them with basil oil.

Heather murmured on her cellphone to her boyfriend Martin, her words indecipherable.

Thoughts raced through Kari's mind, randomly arranged moments that collided into a chaotic mess. She remembered finding Lori Grove's name written in a book as a child and cherishing that single page like some kind of hidden treasure. She would have given anything to know her mother. But not the mother that had angrily taken possession of her body. Never had her fantasies included anything close to an angry ghost.

Kari remembered falling in dance lessons and doodling in her science textbook. She'd gotten in trouble for both. Connie had locked her in her room for failing to live up to expectations after a parent-teacher meeting in which Mrs. Conradie ratted her out. She'd spent hours with her face pressed into the door frame, trying to see out.

She remembered Connie's words. *"I should have smothered you that first night in your crib and saved myself a lifetime of heartache and pain."*

Kari traced the circular pattern of symbols on the blue cloth with her eyes, noting how they matched the symbols embossed on the front of the padded leather book cover. Her grandmother had spent a lifetime berating her, even accusing her of killing her grandfather with cheeseburgers, when all along, it was most likely Connie who had caused his heart problems.

"You would not have been my first choice in heirs."

Well, Connie, Kari thought at the memory, *you would not have been my first choice of grandmothers.*

What was it she'd been thinking about at the funeral? She'd been drinking all day, and her mind had fixated on those words. The memory came back to her now.

Legacy. Duty. Disappointment. Blame.

But not love.

Oh, how she wanted love in her life.

Kari glanced at Angel. He stood close to her, watching the blueberry muffin in her hand as if he silently willed her to eat it. Vivien had sent him to find sugar, and he'd returned with one of the muffins Sue had brought from the coffee shop. She took a bite off the top. Angel gave a small nod.

No, not just love. Family. She wanted a real family.

"Since we know his name now, do you think we can séance my father later?" Kari looked around the room.

Heather and Vivien shared a look.

"Uh, maybe, if he's still around," Heather said. "I haven't seen him. The best thing is for him to have moved on."

"We should concentrate on tonight," Vivien answered. "One ghost at a time."

"Or two," Heather corrected. "Connie and Lori."

"Is it a good idea to put them in the same room?" Angel asked. "I mean, they're not exactly getting along. What if they attack each other?"

"Lori should be weakened from her tirade," Heather said. "Now is the perfect time. We might be able to get her to listen as we talk to Connie. With luck, we can help her heal and move on."

"It will help me to see them together," Vivien said. "I should be able to sense more of what's happening with them."

"There's a lot of family drama to unpack," Kari muttered. "I don't know if one séance will do it."

"I'm sorry I burned the last casserole, though it might be a blessing in disguise." Lorna entered the storage room carrying a white paper bag. "I think it was like turkey and dry stuffing mix and taco seasoning hidden under a ton of cheese. Another just came out of the oven if anyone is hungry. Breakfast one—eggs, sausage, bacon, cheese, shredded hash browns."

"Maybe later," Vivien dismissed.

Lorna had only burned the first casserole because they'd been busy dealing with Kari's possession at the time. The cut on Lorna's forehead caused a wave of guilt to wash over Kari.

"Why don't you let me have that?" Kari offered, touching her own forehead.

"You're not the one who threw me into the door," Lorna answered by way of denial. "I'm a fast healer. Save your strength. Eat that muffin."

Kari took another bite.

Lorna took another muffin out of her bag and gave it to Angel, ordering, "You too. Eat up."

"All right, I need you all to listen up," Heather said. She slid her phone into her back pocket. "Wait. Where's Sue?"

"Here." Sue appeared in the doorway holding the comforter from the guest room. Lorna tried to give her a muffin. "No thanks, already had two."

"Me." Vivien held up her hands, and Lorna tossed it at her.

Seeing Kari looking at the comforter, Sue glanced at Angel and then said, "You know, just in case Angel needs to grab hold of you again."

"Okay, we need everyone to pay attention tonight," Heather said, catching the blueberry muffin Lorna tossed to her. "I know it's late and you might be a little tired after a long day, but I need you to remain vigilant. The spirits we're communicating with are ill-tempered. Their energy could part the veil just enough to draw angry spirits through if we're not vigilant. If I tell you to do something, I need you to do it."

Heather acted like she spoke to everyone, but she gave a pointed look at Kari and Angel.

Angel nodded. "You got it. You're the boss."

Kari frowned. "Do you mean demons? Like what happened with Lorna?"

"More or less," Vivien said.

"Finish that muffin," Lorna ordered Kari.

Kari took another bite, not feeling like food at the moment but they all insisted the sugar would help.

Kari saw the stress Vivien and Lorna were trying to hide in their tense expressions. Heather wore it on her furrowed brow. Sue nervously tapped her fingers against her leg. They finished eating and threw the muffin papers into the bag before forming a circle around the blanket.

"All right, show time." Vivien clapped her hands.

Angel gave Kari an encouraging smile as they joined the circle around the séance book. She stood across from Heather and slowly nodded that she was ready.

"Our intent is to talk to Lori and Connie Grove," Heather stated, holding hands with Sue and Vivien.

Sue reached for Lorna, Lorna for Angel, and Vivien took Kari's hand.

Kari looked up at Angel. "Are you ready?"

He nodded and took her hand in his. The moment they touched, the candles magically lit themselves.

Like before, when they all joined together, she detected the other's emotions as if their spirits melded into hers. A tingling sensation made goosebumps form over her entire body and her hair lifted from her shoulders with a static electric charge. A pulse of energy shot out from her ring finger. At first, the combined feelings were a jumbled mess, and Kari couldn't discern which belonged to whom. She tried to concentrate as she looked at Heather across from her. The woman was more worried about performing this séance than she let on. In fact, they all were.

Kari looked up at Angel. His feelings flooded into her, flowing through their connected hands. Behind the apprehension, she detected something more. His emotions went beyond friendship and concern. She felt his fascination with her, his excitement when he looked at her, his desire to kiss her. For a long moment, she gazed up at him, basking in his feelings as they amplified her own.

"Uh-hem," Lorna cleared her throat. From her suddenly amused expression, it was easy to see what feeling they were picking up from Kari.

"You know we can all feel that, right?" Vivien chuckled.

Kari blinked rapidly in surprise. "Oh, ah..."

"Don't apologize for finding love," Vivien said.

"There really are no secrets in this group, are there?" Kari muttered.

"Never are in families," Lorna said.

The offhand comment wasn't meant as anything

more than an observation, and yet Kari's mind clung to that one word. Family.

The overhead lights flashed and popped, darkening as the bulbs went out. Kari tensed, turning her full attention to the séance book. Moonlight from the window revealed the depths of the shadows. She felt the energy building in the room like an oncoming thunderstorm.

"Let's do this," Vivien said.

"We open the door between two worlds to call forth the spirits of Lori and Connie Grove." The other ladies chanted in unison. Kari mumbled along with them a second behind their words. When she glanced at Angel, he didn't even pretend to speak. "Come back from the grave so that we may hear. Come back from the grave and show yourself to us so that all may see. Come back from the grave and answer for what you have done so that you may be judged."

Tiny flashes of light swarmed over the book before pouring to the side as if their chaotic numbers became trapped within a pair of see-through legs. The candle flames grew taller than should have been possible to reflect within a translucent body. This ghost did not manifest like Julia.

Light moved up the ghostly bodies, continuing upward to reveal Lori standing in a hospital gown. It filled her transparent form. Her shoulders slumped forward, and her head hung as if she had little energy. A steady hum of rage came off her body.

"She's still in the hospital gown," Lorna observed.

"It's how she died," Heather said.

"Is that blood pooling by her feet?" Sue asked.

Kari held her breath. Her mother looked up at her, dead eyes staring as if they didn't see. Kari couldn't look away.

"Why isn't she doing anything?" Kari asked.

"She's still recovering from possessing you. This is good. It's what we wanted." Heather shared a private look with Vivien and nodded. "What do you feel?"

"So much anger," Vivien whispered, a tear slipping down her face. "Forty years trapped in this room, alone and in pain, taken from the man she loves, taken from her baby, deprived of a future, robbed of happiness and love, tortured by those home movies like some kind of prisoner until she had nothing left but agony and fury. Vengeful spirits have been made out of less."

"Mom?" Kari asked. "Can you see me? It's your daughter, Kari."

Lori didn't move, just continued to stare. A soft and slow *fwap, fwap, fwap* sounded only to fade, a sad echo that said more than Lori ever could.

The light split off in another direction, illuminating a second pair of legs.

"Here comes grandma." Heather kept her tone low.

Connie appeared the same way as her daughter, lights dancing until they blended into high-waisted pants and a silk shirt with bold paisley patterns. She looked younger than when she died with full hair and makeup. Trust Connie to be vain, even in death.

"Remain calm," Heather said quietly, dropping Sue and Vivien's hands.

"You can let go," Lorna whispered to Kari. "Once they manifest, we don't need to remain joined. The magic is already happening. Breaking contact won't scare them away."

Kari nodded, but it took a few more seconds before she could loosen the tight grip she had on Lorna's fingers. When she tried to release Angel, he didn't want to let her go.

"Viv?" Lorna prompted.

Vivien shifted her attention to Connie and shivered. She rubbed her arms. "This one is a chilling vortex of control and need. There's this..."

"What?" Angel asked.

Connie's spirit looked at Lori's and smiled.

"Pettiness." Vivien frowned as if trying to find the right words. "Smugness. Self-satisfaction at—*oh, no.*"

Kari watched the color drain from Vivien's face. "What? Tell me."

The vibration coming from the ring grew, causing her hand to shake. She looked at the other women. They had the same reaction.

"Connie's happy Lori is caged like a supernatural zoo animal. She thinks she's justified in trapping her daughter's spirit in some kind of ultimate I-told-you-so." Vivien took a deep breath. "I don't want to feel this. It's like looking into the heart of..."

"What?" Kari insisted.

"The projector wasn't to draw Lori's spirit here so that she could bind her to the room. It was meant to torture her as part of something with six spells," Vivien said.

"That's specific," Heather said.

Vivien rubbed her ring finger before lifting her hands toward the ghosts. "I can feel her here, like some timeless battle. Connie wanted her to think about what she'd done wrong."

"Wrong?" Lorna asked.

"Defying her mother's wishes," Kari explained, not needing Vivien's psychic abilities to know the answer. "What do you mean by six spells?"

Vivien didn't have time to answer.

Suddenly, Connie solidified more than before though she remained transparent. She laughed and looked at the blue cloth they had manifested on. She turned in a small circle without moving past the symbols that were supposed to lock her inside. Connie's heeled shoes made no noise though Kari remembered the sound of them clicking on floors just like this one.

"Julia, seriously? A binding séance?" Connie turned her attention to her summoners, leaning to look past Lori's motionless form to Sue. When Sue stepped back, Connie laughed harder. "Is this the best you could scrounge up? I'm rather insulted by this second-rate shitshow."

Angel's fingers worked against hers. Kari didn't dare take her eyes away from her grandmother.

Connie turned to Heather and Vivien. "Well, where are you? Don't try to hide."

"Julia's not here." Heather pressed her finger to her temple as if fighting a sudden headache.

"Ah, that's right. She's dead." Connie patted her hair as if to push the short locks into place.

"So are you," Heather countered.

"Not for long," Connie quipped.

"You need to face reality," Sue said. "You're dead. Time to make amends and move on."

"You have to deal with us," Vivien added.

"You have a lot to answer for," Lorna said.

Connie snorted as she glanced over Lorna.

"Ooo, I'm scared," Connie mocked, throwing up her hands and forcing a shiver. "I see you have one of Julia's little decoder rings too. Fat little good it did my daughter."

Connie's eyes finally landed on Kari, and she began to smile. However, when she saw her granddaughter holding hands with Angel, the expression turned sour.

"You can't be serious," Connie snapped. "Your grandfather is turning over in his grave."

Kari had not missed that condescending tone.

"Stop that at once. I forbid you from forming a relationship with this..." Connie gestured her hand at Angel. "Just no. We don't have time for this."

"Connie, this is Angel," Kari introduced. "He's..."

She glanced at Angel, wondering what label to put on them. Her hand trembled in his, and he held it tighter.

"I'm her boyfriend and lover," Angel filled in. "I'm crazy about your granddaughter."

Connie visibly shuddered.

"Ha!" Vivien laughed at the reaction. "She didn't like that."

"Doesn't matter," Kari said to Angel. "I liked it."

"Sorry, I couldn't resist," he answered. "She's a piece of work."

Connie's spirit charged the invisible barrier created by Julia's symbols. Her face distorted and blurred at the movement. Kari leaped back, trying to pull Angel with her. He automatically tried to shield her behind him.

The magical protection flung the spirit back before she could reach them, but it did not stop Connie's anger. "I will not be judged by some peasant!"

Kari's heart pounded in fright. She pushed past Angel and marched to face Connie. "Stop it!"

Connie laughed, the sound grating. "Or what?"

"This is taking a lot of energy," Heather said, holding her head. "You might want to say what you need to before we have nothing left."

"How could you?" Kari asked Connie, shaking her head.

She realized it was a vague question. Connie needed to account for so much.

"You stole my eggs and made me a mother. You hexed my parents." Kari pointed at her mom's floating figure. Lori continued to stare, dead-eyed. "Your spell killed my mom. We found your notebook. You probably killed your husband, and God knows who else."

"Your father killed your mother," Connie countered. Age melted from her face, and she looked more like she did when she'd stood in this very room and cursed her daughter. "I warned him to stay away, but he just had to have her. Stupid money-grubbing little punk."

"They loved each other," Kari countered. She'd seen it in her mother's memories. They might have been young and daydreamers, but they deserved a chance to be happy and together.

"Love is the emotion of idiots." Connie went to stand in front of Lori. She crossed her arms over her chest. "He is beneath our family. I told her that. If she had been a good girl, she would be standing there," she glanced at Kari, "not you."

The words stung.

"Wait, *is* or *was*?" Lorna interrupted. "You said he *is* beneath our family, not was."

Connie's eyes widened, and she looked around. "Ah, no."

"Is her father still alive?" Heather asked.

"What did you do, Connie?" Kari demanded. Her heart hammered violently, and she found it difficult to breathe. Could it be true? Could her father still be alive? She'd never confirmed the story of the bus accident. And it wouldn't be beneath Connie to lie.

"Calm down," Connie waved in dismissal.

Lori's head tilted to the side, and her hand twitched, the first sign of awareness since she materialized. Connie didn't notice.

"Where is he?" Vivien asked. "You owe her that much. Where's Derek Miller?"

"Gone," Connie said. "And he won't come anywhere near you."

Her father was alive. She'd find him.

"It doesn't matter," Connie said. "It's going to take a few generations for the bloodline to be cleansed of—"

"Shut up!" Kari yelled.

"Now you get a backbone," Connie mocked. "Are you sure you don't need your mommy to use you as a vessel first?"

Lori's head twitched, and she stared at Connie.

"If you have something to say, say it. After today I'm not going to séance you again." Kari felt Angel standing behind her. Lorna smiled and nodded in encouragement. Heather held her head with one hand, thumb pressed into her temple, and stared forward. Sue and Vivien quietly watched.

"You're weak and pathetic. You couldn't even defend yourself against a dying woman. You had to have your mommy come and save you." Connie shook her head in disgust.

"Just stop with all your hate, you miserable bitch," Kari said. "I have news for you. I'm going to find Constance, and I'm going to raise her in the RV. She's going to travel everywhere and meet everyone, and she's going to make friends with people who are the complete opposite of you."

Connie's form shimmered and aged. Wrinkles spread from her eyes and lips and trailed along her cheeks. "You'll never find her in time."

The threat left Kari cold. "In time for what?"

"That kid is going to grow up without you, and the day she turns eighteen, she will legally take over the entire estate." Connie glided more than walked to stand before Kari. "Oh? Did you not get to that part of the will with the lawyer? Surprise! You're not even a trustee."

"You're lying," Kari denied. "The lawyer already gave me the paperwork, and quite frankly, you could have left your chicken farm and tobacco company to charity for all I care. I never asked for any of it."

Connie laughed and looked way too smug.

"Tell me where Constance is. No more games." Kari wanted this to be over. Connie had managed to extinguish any feelings of regret and love Kari might have felt for her. Betrayal piled on betrayals until all that was left was a hollow feeling in the pit of her stomach.

"I'm not talking about some old stocks and real estate. I'm talking about the family fortune, all six hundred million."

Kari's eyes widened. The lawyer had told her two million in various assets. "You didn't have six hundred million. Stop with your stories. No one here cares."

"Yeah, I didn't think so." Connie's features became younger as if she couldn't decide on which version of herself that she wanted to be. Her clothes tightened into an A-line skirt and fitted blouse.

"You're lying." Kari lifted her hands. "And I don't care if you're not. I don't want your—"

"Oh, shit!" Vivien exclaimed. "Mom's awake."

Lori's head jerked, and her eyes narrowed in on Connie.

Fwap-fwap.

The soft noise was the only sound Lori made.

Connie's expression seemed to soften as she walked toward Lori. She reached her hand and let it hover by her face. "You're not looking well, dear."

Lori's body flickered and became brighter.

Kari moved around the circle to better watch them.

Fwap-fwap.

"Use your words," Connie encouraged. For a brief moment, she sounded like a mother and not the monster she had been in life.

"Leave," Lori grunted. "Alone."

"I know. I left you alone," Connie said.

Lori gave a stiff shake of her head. "Leave. Alone."

"You want me to leave you alone now?" Connie dropped her hands. "Sorry, Lori. You know what they say. You reap what you sow."

Lori twitched again. Her eyes darted to Kari and then back. "Leave. Alone."

"Oh, don't you worry. I'll leave your daughter alone. All alone." Connie smiled, and the monster showed in that expression.

"Leave!" Lori charged Connie, slamming into her and sweeping her violently into the invisible boundary.

Connie yelped in surprise as her body hit the wall of their cell. She dissipated into a puff of dark smoke.

Kari held her breath, watching for what her mother would do next. Her image flickered, and for a moment, she worried Lori might disappear too.

Lori's hospital gown blurred into a sundress as she turned. She stared at Kari as she crossed the circle to come near. Her body brightened as if some of the anger went away.

"I'm sorry, baby," Lori whispered. Only the eyes

showed Lori's true years. Her youthful face appeared frozen in time and had been spared the knowledge of wrinkles and age spots. There was an innate tragedy in one dying so young.

"It's not your fault," Kari answered. Her mother looked like a scared teenager who needed to be comforted. "I know you tried to leave here and start a new life."

Fwap-fwap…

The sundress changed into the hospital gown, and Lori's rage returned. Her skin grayed. When she spoke, the tone churned with gravel. "I'm sorry I didn't get to her sooner."

Kari had imagined talking to her mother in so many ways, so many conversations, and talking about murdering Connie had never been one of them.

Lori's sundress came back and the sound of the projector stopped. "She wants to take the baby."

"It doesn't matter now. I'm here. I'm okay." Kari lifted her hand toward her mother. "I'm safe."

"Don't," Vivien instructed when Kari would reach past the circle of symbols. "She's unstable. Don't give her vengeful spirit a bridge into you."

"She's not a vengeful spirit." Kari saw the face of a young teenager. "She's just a confused kid."

"The baby." Lori's face wavered in transparency,

becoming brighter and fading like waves washing across a sandy shore. "Take it as her own."

"Mom, I'm all right," Kari insisted. "I survived Connie. I'm happy now. Everything is going to be all right. I'll find my father. I'll find Derek. I'll tell him what Connie did."

"Derek?" Lori smiled, and her clothing shifted into the dinosaur shirt she'd been wearing on Derek's bed. Just as quickly, the hospital gown replaced it and her features darkened. "She kills everything she touches."

"What's wrong with her?" Kari asked. "Why does she keep changing like this? Can't we do something?"

"She's unstable." Vivien rubbed small circles over Kari's back as if to comfort her. "Connie spent decades torturing her. That kind of pain is all-consuming."

"She wants to take the place of the soul," Lori insisted. "You can't let her."

"Mom, I'm—"

"Don't let her take the soul," Lori pleaded.

"Okay, we won't," Heather answered. "I promise, Lori, we'll make sure Connie never takes anything again."

Lori calmed, again finding her dinosaur shirt. Her eyes softened. "You look like Derek. He loved you before he even met you."

A tremor worked over Kari, and she tried not to cry.

"Derek looked at me the way this one looks at you," Lori continued, smiling at Angel. "It reminds me of a dance, the music you want to last forever, the melancholy and longing when it's over."

"Mom, I'm so sorry this happened to you. I'm sorry I never got the chance to know you." Kari again tried to reach forward, and Vivien blocked her hand.

"You know me." Lori smiled and placed her fingers over her chest, and they seemed to dip below the surface to where her heart would have been. "You have me here. The rest are just fleeting moments—a dance. In the end, only the feeling it gives you matters, not the lyrics. Your parents love you. That is what will linger. That is everything."

Lori flashed into her hospital gown and then back into the sundress. The contrasting darkness and lightness of the personalities were vastly different. Waves of rage and love alternated between the two. Kari's hand vibrated from the ring, amplifying her feelings.

"Mom, stay with me." Kari started to lift her hand again, but this time it was her mother's look that stopped her.

"Your friend is right." Lori became more see-through. "The rage will take us both. I never wanted to hurt anyone. You can't let me out. I'm too tired to fight it."

"I don't want to trap you," Kari denied. "What Connie did—"

Lori flickered again, through rage and love and then desperation. She ended up in the dinosaur shirt. "Release me. Please. You have to let me go. I don't want to hurt anyone else."

"But you just said not to let you leave." Kari looked at the others in confusion. "I don't understand."

Sue and Lorna stayed quiet, standing close together. Lorna gave her a kind, sad smile of encouragement. Heather hadn't moved as she watched from the other side of the blue cloth. She felt more than saw Angel standing behind her. Vivien had her hand on her wrist, holding it as she stayed close.

"You have to let me go," Lori repeated.

"I just found you." Kari shook her head. "I have so many questions. I want to know everything about you. I want to tell you about me."

"Oh, baby, that's not how life works. You don't always find answers." Lori flickered again, this time locking in rage. Her hair hung around her face as she stood in her hospital gown.

A soft *fwap-fwap-fwap* followed this version of Lori as if to remind her of her torment.

"Mom?" Kari looked at Vivien in desperation. "How do we get her to stop doing that?"

"We can't," Heather answered. "She's slipping, turning completely into a vengeful spirit. She's asking us to save her soul before the hatred takes over completely."

"Mom, can you understand me?" Kari leaned over, trying to make Lori look at her. "I love you. I'm sorry this happened."

Lori flickered to the sundress. "I love you, my sweet baby."

"Do you know where Connie hid my daughter?" Kari asked.

Lori shook her head and warned, "Don't let her take the soul."

"You said that before," Vivien stated. "Do you mean your granddaughter's soul? Does Connie want to use the baby for something?"

"Please," Lori begged, her image becoming a blur of sundress, dinosaur, and hospital gown. She cried out and clutched her stomach. "Please release me."

"I don't want to let her go," Kari whispered. Tears streamed down her face.

"She's in pain," Vivien answered. "Don't you want to help her?"

Kari nodded. Of course, she wanted to help her.

She also wanted to hug her and keep talking to her. "Mom, I love you."

She felt Vivien take her hand. Lorna appeared and took her other one. Angel touched her shoulder from behind. Heather came around to stand between Sue and Lorna.

"I'm sorry this happened to you, Lori. But hopefully, you'll find peace now," Heather said.

Then as if an unspoken plan, the other women began to speak in unison. "Spirit, you have been found pure. We release you into the light. Go in peace and love."

Kari gasped for air, unable to speak past the pain in her chest.

Lori smiled in relief. A few lights danced over her like the dying embers of a bonfire. The spirit tilted her head back and closed her eyes.

"Goodbye, mom," Kari whispered.

The lights intensified as Lori dissolved into thousands of sparkling pieces, only to disappear.

The air in the room instantly felt lighter, free from the rage and pain of before. The candle flames lowered to a soft burn, and the overhead lights did not turn back on.

"She's gone," Heather said. "You did the right thing

in letting her go. It wouldn't have worked if you were selfish and made her stay."

"That was incredibly brave of you," Sue said.

"I'm proud of you," Lorna added. "I know that wasn't easy."

Kari felt more drained than she had ever been in her life. She stared at the empty cloth.

"She needs rest," Vivien stated. "It's late. Connie burned a lot of energy. I don't think we need to worry about her for a while. We'll talk about all of this in the morning."

"Come on, Kari," Angel prompted, slipping his arm around her to support her as he urged her to walk with him out of the storage room. "You look like you're about to pass out."

"Will you stay with me tonight?" she asked. "I don't want to be alone."

"I have nowhere else I'd rather be," he answered. "Where do you want to sleep?"

Instead of answering, Kari felt light flash as she delivered them into the RV.

Angel softly chuckled as he moved aside so that she could crawl onto the bed. "RV it is. Do you want me to get you something to eat or drink?"

"No," she reached for him in the shadows. When her mother had disappeared, it felt like every last bit of her energy had gone with her, and Kari could barely keep her eyes open. "Right now, I just want the world to stop moving, so I can sleep."

Angel crawled next to her on the bed and held her. As she drifted to sleep, she heard him whisper, "All I want right now is to be with you."

CHAPTER SIXTEEN

FOUR DAYS PASSED IN A FOG, and Kari felt her time marked by casseroles and tears and frustrations. Freeing her mother's spirit felt more like a loss than Connie's funeral. What little comfort she could take in knowing her mother had moved on to the next phase of her eternity was undone by the knowledge that she had a daughter and father out there in the world.

Broccoli casserole. Did her father know about her? Why had he stayed away?

Ranch chicken casserole. Did her daughter know about her? What had Connie told her?

Taco casserole. Why couldn't they séance Connie back? What did she have planned for Constance?

Tuna noodle casserole. By all that was holy, enough with the fucking casseroles already.

"I've got tacos. I've got cheeseburgers. I've got fries," Vivien announced, coming into the house without knocking. She made her way to the dining room carrying two sizable fast-food bags in her arms.

The ladies had started to come and go as they pleased. Kari didn't mind, as long as they didn't leave her alone in the house.

Thankfully, she was able to sleep in her RV, often with Angel next to her. If she had her way, she would have never left the bed, but in the mornings, when he got up to work, she was always called back to the empty storage room.

Kari wore jeans, a sweater cardigan over her t-shirt, and tennis shoes. Except when she was making love to Angel, she liked to be fully clothed with her driver's license and bank card in one back pocket and her cellphone in the other. There was always a fear she'd end up naked in the town square, or at the very least, in need of a pair of shoes.

"Burritos," Vivien continued as she set the bags down. "Chicken nuggets. Fish sandwiches. Taquitos. Salad—just kidding. Chocolate cake, strawberry cake, lemon cake, and nachos."

"What? No fried chicken," Kari teased.

Vivien frowned as she glanced at her bags. "I could go—"

"That was a joke," Kari interrupted. "Looks like you got all the major food groups covered."

"I know everyone always means well when they send food to help the family after a funeral, but if we eat another baked mystery meal kitchen experiment, I'm going to have to start fasting," Vivien stated.

Kari gave her a bemused once over. "I don't get how you look like you do and eat like you eat."

"I like to run." Vivien gave a small wave of dismissal. "And that's the true blessing behind Julia's rings. Our powers are like magical liposuction. They suck the fat right off."

"That is not true," Lorna contradicted as she entered the dining room carrying a stack of plates and napkins. "Magic burns carbs."

"Same thing, more or less," Vivien dismissed.

"You're looking better." Lorna gave Kari a kind look, but Kari knew what she really meant was her eyes were not so red from crying, and her body wasn't tense with anger.

"Thanks," Kari answered. "I'm feeling better."

"If you're not one-hundred percent yet, that would be understandable," Lorna continued. "Even without the emotional toll, a possession, summoning two ghosts—"

"Two deeply emotional, draining ghosts," Vivien inserted.

"—the family drama would be enough to make anyone sick," Lorna finished.

"Drama is a kind way of saying it." Kari shook her head when Vivien tried to hand her a taco. She couldn't eat. "Mucky murderous cesspool might be more accurate. Connie killed Lori, vengeful spirit Lori killed Connie, Connie killed my grandfather, and God knows who else. We can't find my daughter or my father. I can't get my mother's warning out of my head that Connie is going to take a soul."

Vivien tossed the taco on the table. "I know. I can't get it out of my head either. I didn't want to say anything until I had something solid, but I have a private investigator trying to find her. He'll be tactful, but he hasn't found anything yet."

"Angel offered to have his cousin look into it. He's an investigator too." Kari looked between Lorna and Vivien. She wanted them to tell her it was all right, that Connie had no history of hurting young children, or that she wouldn't hurt the girl she'd forced into the world.

They said nothing.

"But, I mean, Connie wanted an heir she could be proud of, right?" Kari continued to glance between them. "So she wouldn't actually hurt Constance. My mom probably meant that Connie was raising my daughter with the same soul-sucking coldheartedness that she showed the both of us."

"Yeah, yeah." Lorna nodded.

"Maybe," Vivien said.

Neither looked convinced.

Kari felt tears starting and swiped at them. "What do I do? I can't leave the house. The law office keeps saying they'll call me back. Dr. Spitz and his new Alcott-Grove fertility wing say they have no record of me being a patient. I've tried making myself transport to Constance, but all I managed to do was reappear in the storage room."

"We're not going to pretend to know how your powers work," Lorna soothed, "but if they're tied to your emotions, you're probably too distraught to focus on her. Or you don't have a location to focus on, which might affect where you can go, so it brings you to the closest place it can find. Or maybe it will just happen when it needs—"

A bright light flashed, blinding her to Lorna's face. Kari lifted her hands to protect her eyes. She knew before she lowered them that she had traveled again.

Kari expected to be in the storage room. Instead, a cool breeze blew over her. Her cardigan fluttered behind her. She stood in a field, bathed in bright sunlight.

The view looked familiar, in the way all landscapes started to look familiar after years of traveling. Tall grasses rolled over hills, rippling like waves in the breeze. When she turned, she saw a row of wood fencing, stretching along the back of houses as if to keep them caged away from nature. The uniformed spacing and matching rooflines instantly said it was a planned neighborhood.

Kari had transported alone but wished her friends had come with her. "What now?"

No one answered.

Kari felt her back pocket to ensure her bank card and license were still there before taking her phone. She began walking toward the houses and started to call Vivien. The grasses parted as if an invisible force ran toward her. Kari stopped dialing and held still as she watched it.

Kari's legs tensed, and she got ready to run. An orange kitten leaped out of the grass and pounced toward her foot. She jumped back in surprise to avoid the small paws.

"Oh, hey, where did you come from?" Kari picked up the animal. The kitten only mildly protested as it squirmed into a more comfortable position in her arms.

"Are you lost?"

Kari took a step toward the houses. Lights flashed, and when she could again see, she had moved several yards closer while still holding the kitten. She took another step, and it happened again. The fence was close enough she made out the details of the slats.

The kitten meowed and wiggled playfully. Kari stopped walking and scratched its ears.

"You're a feisty one." She couldn't help her small laugh.

"Cute and fluffy."

The sound of her mother's voice drifted through her mind, reminding her of that first projection she'd watched of Lori twirling in a field. She frowned. Her parents had an orange kitten in a field like this one. She glanced around, half expecting to see the dark image of her father's tall, slender, out-of-focus shape. The landscape remained normal.

Kari still held her phone and finished dialing.

"Where did you go?" Vivien answered almost instantly. "We were about to call you. We didn't see you in the storage room or RV."

"I don't know. I'm in a field with a cat. I think I might be in one of my father's films," she said.

"Is he there?" Vivien sounded concerned.

"I'm alone, well, except for a lost kitten I found."

"Do you see any street signs or landmarks nearby?"

"There are some houses up ahead. I'll see if I can find anyone."

Kari took another step, and again she crossed several yards. Apprehension filled her. What if she'd traveled into the past? What if her teenage parents were here?

"What was that? I can't hear you. You're breaking up." Vivien's voice lifted as she yelled into the phone.

Kari saw a figure nearby. A woman stood with her back to her and her face pressed against the fence. "Stay on the line. I see someone."

She concentrated on taking small steps so as not to transport across the field and scare the woman.

"Hey," Kari called when she was close enough to talk without yelling.

The woman turned, startled. Kari cried out in fright to see Connie. She clutched the kitten to her chest as she stumbled backward. Her phone fell to the ground. The ghost dissipated into smoke and a frigid breeze blasted Kari's skin.

Kari fumbled for her phone, jerking her head back and forth as she watched the landscape for her grandmother. Her heart hammered in her chest, nearly choking her with fright.

"What?" Vivien's voice yelled from the ground.

Kari grabbed her phone, panting, "Connie. Here. Connie."

"You see Connie?" Vivien demanded. Chaotic voices stirred up behind her as Lorna and Heather began asking questions.

"Please come get me," Kari begged into the phone, shivering. "I don't know what I'm—"

The phone beeped and went dead.

"Hello?" Kari cried into the phone, shaking it as if that would make her friend's voice come back. "Vivien? Hello?"

Kari held the kitten close as it tried to play. She trembled as she tried to look around the field. She didn't want to be alone. She didn't know what to do.

"Holy magic mystery transporter ride! What was that?" Lorna exclaimed.

Kari gasped, spinning around at the sound. Lorna, Heather, and Vivien appeared behind her. The women stumbled to find their footing. Seconds later, Sue appeared in the process of pulling down her pants. She fell back on her backside.

"What the...?" Sue cried out in surprise. "What happened to the toilet?"

"Looks like Kari is fine-tuning that traveling power of hers," Vivien answered.

"I didn't mean to," Kari whispered at the same

time. The vibration in her hand from the ring had become a familiar sensation, both a warning and a comfort.

"Here," Vivien offered her hand with a small laugh. "Before you get a grassy ass."

"Too late." Sue tugged on her pants. "I guess I should be thankful I wasn't in the bathtub."

"Or in public," Lorna added. "That would be hard to explain."

"Nope, running around naked would be worse," Sue said.

"I'm—" Kari began to apologize.

"Where are we?" Heather interrupted before nodding toward the kitten. "Cute cat."

"We'll save a bundle on airfare having you in our little magical family," Vivien said. "Did you say you saw Connie?"

"She was..." Kari pointed toward the fence.

"Heather?" Lorna prompted.

Heather looked around. "I don't see Connie. I do see a pioneer woman and what looks to be two teenagers. They're in an old loop. They don't notice us." She took a deep, steadying breath. "And now they're gone."

Kari followed her gaze and briefly wondered at the

many sad events Heather must have had cause to witness in her life.

"Here, give that little floofy to me." Lorna took the cat from her.

"This looks like the kitten my mother showed me in her home movies. Then I see Connie there." Kari again pointed toward the fence. Having her friends with her for support allowed her to breathe easier. The realization was strange, considering she was used to being alone.

"Then that's the way we go," Heather said.

"I really hope that way has a restroom," Sue muttered.

"Sorry about that," Kari said.

"Yeah, let's see what Creepy Connie was peeping at." Vivien strode next to Heather toward the houses.

"That's not your cat," a young voice said from beyond the fence.

Kari gasped to hear the girl and blurted, "Constance? Is that you?"

Who else could it be?

"You can't keep Jingles," the girl insisted. "He's not supposed to be out there."

"Is your name Constance?" Kari asked, going to the fence to look between the slats until she found a young girl peeking out at them. She sunk to her knees to be more on the girl's level. A brown eye met hers. They were inches apart but blocked by wood.

Kari felt her breath bouncing back against her face and remembered peeking through the crack of a door as a child, and more recently, when she first saw her mother.

"I'm not supposed to talk to strangers," the girl answered.

"That's good advice," Kari said.

"But I have to talk to you because you have Jingles, and he's not yours," she said. "And you know my name."

Constance. Her daughter.

"Whose is he?" Kari reached her fingers between the wood, drawn to touch her.

"Mrs. Brown. She lets me babysit him."

"Is that your neighbor?" Her fingertips didn't reach far.

"My caretaker," Constance answered. "One of them. She is in charge of my dietary plan."

"Can we bring him around to you?" Lorna asked.

Constance disappeared.

"No, wait," Kari said, moving to follow the girl. She watched her shadow move along the slats.

Constance pushed aside a piece of wood to create a small hole. A hand came through. "You can put him through here. He likes to get out of the yard and run around. He always comes back when I call him."

Kari's hand shook as she reached for her daughter. Her fingers brushed the palm. Energy pulsed through the ring.

"That tickles." Constance's fingers curled, and she patted the ground. "Come here, Jingles."

Kari let her hand hover, not wanting to be some weird stranger while resisting the urge to grab hold.

"Here." Lorna handed Kari the cat.

Kari placed the animal on the ground and let her fingers touch the child briefly. Jingles scampered through the hole. Kari leaned her face close to the ground to look inside. The girl's sneaker planted on the ground as she stood, and the piece of wood slid over the hole.

"No, wait," Kari tried to push the wood over, but Constance placed a brick in front of it. "I just want to talk to you."

"Mr. Gunderson will be here soon."

"Oh, yeah?" Kari asked, pressing her face against the slats. "Who's that?"

"He checks my blood," Constance said nonchalantly.

"Are you sick?" Kari crawled along the fence, trying to watch.

"No." Constance scoffed as if it were a ridiculous question.

Kari heard more than saw her run toward the house. "No, wait."

"Kari, come on," Vivien said, pulling at her arm to get her off the ground. "We'll find a way around."

Kari pulled on one of the wood slats trying to break it. "We found her. I need to get—"

"Whoa, easy, you don't want to scare her," Lorna tried to block Kari's hands.

"Or get arrested," Sue added.

When they tried to hold her back, Kari transported herself to the other side of the fence. The backyard was set up like a kid-sized obstacle course with balance beams, hurdles, arches, rings, and a climbing wall. Manicured grass grew around worn dirt paths as if someone had spent hours upon hours running through the different stations. Constance had gone inside. Kari wanted to go after her.

"Kari?" Heather whispered. "What do you see?"

"Um." Kari frowned. "Mini-military training? Some kind of fitness course."

This didn't feel like the kind of education Connie would insist on. Athleticism was usually encouraged in the form of ballet and archery.

"Do you see any ghosts?" Heather insisted.

Kari glanced over the empty backyard. Wooden fences lined both sides to keep the neighbors out. "No."

Even as she said it, Connie appeared under the monkey bars. The moment was brief then she disappeared.

Kari wanted her friends with her, and they suddenly appeared by her side.

"Oh! A little warning next time," Sue said, holding her stomach and breathing heavily.

"It feels like when we traveled through the house during the storm," Vivien said before adding playfully, "Kari must like us. She doesn't want us to leave her."

Vivien tried to lighten with humor often.

"I do like you," Kari answered matter-of-factly before gesturing toward the monkey bars. "Connie was there a few seconds ago."

"She's there now." Heather nodded toward the back door. "I don't think she sees us."

"Should we go back and contain her with a séance? Get her away from Constance?" Lorna asked.

"Kari's magic chose now to bring us to Constance." Heather kept her eyes on the house. "We're meant to be here."

"I don't want to leave her," Kari said. The panic inside her was like nothing she'd ever felt. Seeing the girl—*her daughter*—alive and talking, even if it was just an eye, a hand, a foot, through a fence, shook her to the core. Knowing she had a kid wasn't the same as hearing that small matter-of-fact voice. The sensations running up her arm from her hand intensified. "I don't know where we are. We need to get her. I want to transport to her. Why is my magic not bringing me to her?"

"It is. It did," Heather answered. "We're here."

The magical sensations felt stronger as they continued to grow.

"Let's go around front and knock," Lorna said.

"Let's sneak in the back," Vivien countered. "No need to announce ourselves.

"If we go in there, they might call the police on us," Sue said.

"I don't care." Kari moved toward the back door.

"Wait, I'll go in first," Sue suggested. "I'll create a distraction. Just bail me out later if it comes to it."

Kari didn't listen as she opened the back door.

"Or not," Sue said.

Kari stood quietly in the kitchen as the others joined her. No item was out of place in the immaculate home. A chalkboard on the wall had a list of times next to food and exercises. Jars and bottles stood like good little soldiers next to a blender on the center island. Laminated sheets of paper were set out in front of them.

"These are smoothie recipes," Lorna said quietly, touching one of the sheets. "Not very good ones." She lifted one of the jars and read "calcium powder" before setting it back down.

"Do you see Connie?" Kari asked.

Heather shook her head in denial.

"Vitamin D supplement, whey protein," Lorna continued reading labels.

"Connie used to hire nutritionists for me all the time, but never to this extreme. She thought it could help boost my focus and make me smarter. My grandfather and I would sneak cheeseburgers. It was one of the few things we did together," Kari said. Though there was small comfort in knowing the girl was safe, she needed to get Constance out of there.

"We'll get her," Vivien touched her arm, answering Kari's unspoken thought.

Heather checked the doorway leading out of the kitchen. "I don't hear anyone."

Power suddenly surged up her hand like a strike of lightning, causing her arm to jerk.

"You're early," a stern voice said from behind Kari.

They startled and turned in surprise from where they'd been watching Heather.

A resolute woman in nursing scrubs shut the small door that Kari had dismissed as a pantry. She walked toward the blender. The severe expression appeared etched into her face as if her face never cracked a smile. Her hair was pulled back into a bun.

"I thought they were sending three of you. Someone would have called you with the results of today's blood tests." The woman barely glanced at the laminated sheets as she began measuring and pouring ingredients into the blender. "The transplant isn't scheduled until later today."

Transplant? Kari gasped, but Vivien shook her head and lifted a hand, silently telling her not to speak.

"I am Mrs. Willow," the woman continued. "You may call me Mrs. Willow. Behind me, you will find the showers and fresh uniforms. Everyone must be decontaminated before their shifts. All exposures are controlled. I assume you all have your medical clearance?"

"Uh—" Kari began.

"Yes," Vivien answered. "We've all been cleared."

"Good. I assume it's been explained you won't be paid if you get her sick." When no one answered, Mrs. Willow glanced at Vivien.

"Yes," Vivien answered again. "We've been informed."

"Good." Mrs. Willow nodded and continued loading items into the blender. "It's not my job to babysit you. Employee lunches are labeled in the fridge. Do not share them. You do not touch anything in the green containers. If you make a mess, clean it up. I am not working for you. I am required to remind you of your Non-Disclosure Agreements."

"Thank you, Mrs. Willow." Vivien led the way to the door from which Mrs. Willow had entered. She grabbed Kari's arm as she passed, dragging her behind her.

The not-the-pantry door led to a narrow hallway and opened to a sparse locker room with showers. Disinfectants scented the air, causing each breath to burn just a little.

"What kind of sci-fi setup is this?" Heather asked.

"Thank God, a bathroom," Sue said, hurrying toward a stall.

"It looks like the CDC came and set up a medical command center." Lorna went to the rack of blue nursing scrubs that matched the ones Mrs. Willow wore. They hung next to a wall of shoe cubbies filled with white sneakers labeled with several sizes.

"Do you think Constance is sick? They said she needed a transplant. That would explain the blood test and all the health food." Kari's hands shook. She didn't know what to do. "I want to get her out of here with every fiber of my being, but if she's not well or if she needs medical care…"

"She didn't seem sick to me," Vivien said. "Normally, I can sense those things."

Kari looked around the sterile environment, unconvinced.

"If she is, I'll help her," Lorna assured Kari. "We'll find a way to heal her."

"There was something off about Mrs. Willow, but if she's going to let us roam the halls, then I say everyone gets in the shower, put on some scrubs, and," Vivien placed her hand on Kari's shoulder, "let's go bring your daughter home."

CHAPTER SEVENTEEN

KARI TRIED to control her breathing as they walked through the kitchen into the home. She felt a wet curl tickling the back of her neck as it escaped the bun. Mrs. Willow was not the only employee roaming the house. Several housekeepers moved through the home, performing various tasks. They all wore matching blue scrubs and white shoes.

"What the hell is this place?" Kari whispered to Heather. "Some kind of cult?"

They passed a housekeeper dusting. Lorna began to reach for her to tap her arm.

"Not her," Vivien whispered.

Lorna dropped her hand.

Another housekeeper carried a load of laundry toward the stairs. Sue motioned toward her.

"Not her." Vivien then nodded toward the woman washing windows. "That one."

They approached the woman.

"Excuse me," Kari said. "Where is Constance?"

The woman looked confused.

"The little girl," Heather prompted.

"Oh." The window washer nodded to the stairs. "The ward is in her room."

"Thank you," Heather answered as Kari made a move to run toward the stairs.

Vivien grabbed her arm. "Keep calm. Don't draw notice."

"One step at a time," Heather added.

Kari nodded. It took everything in her not to sprint up the stairs and tear down every door.

When they reached the second-story landing, the sound of cartoons came from the end of the hall. Not seeing any workers, Kari rushed toward the sound.

A chalkboard hung on the hallway wall outlining a schedule. The day alternated between physical exercise and playtime with a few meals thrown in and a medical check.

"Heather? Anything?" Vivien asked.

"No. I don't see Connie," Heather answered.

"This isn't right." Kari pointed at the chalkboard.

"This isn't Connie. Where are the math tutors and ballet lessons, and *français* lessons? When I was six, I had three tutors and a slew of activities. She didn't even let me take a break when I had the flu. What are these people doing here? None of this feels right. Connie would never allow this."

"I agree," Vivien said. "Everything I've felt from Connie, everything you've told us, this doesn't make sense."

"Do you think it's because she needs a transplant?" Lorna asked. "Maybe I can do something for her."

Kari listened to the sound of cartoons before opening the door without knocking. She peeked inside at a pink bedroom.

"I'm telling you that doesn't make sense. When we were outside, I didn't get the impression she was sick," Vivien said. "Just a little sad and lonely."

"Sue, Lorna, can you stand lookout?" Heather asked. "I'll watch for Connie."

"Yeah," Sue answered.

"Viv, do your thing," Heather encouraged. "We don't want to scare the child."

Kari said nothing as she went inside. She expected there to be learning centers and educational posters on the wall. Instead, she found toys, tea sets, stuffed animals, dollhouses, and a rocking horse. The room would be any little girl's dream. Heck, it would have been Kari's dream as a child. She had the learning centers and the endless tutors. None of this made sense. There were too many toys and not enough textbooks.

"I have fifteen more minutes," Constance said from her place on the floor, not turning around. She sat in front of a television, watching cartoon animals chase each other around. Mrs. Willow's health shake sat next to her, half empty. No one else was in the room.

Constance's brown hair had been pulled back into a bun to match the rest of the female staff, but Kari detected a wayward curl trying to sneak free at the nape of her neck. Someone had dressed her in mini-scrubs so she'd look like everyone else.

"I'm allowed to watch the whole thing," Constance added.

Kari slowly crossed the bedroom to get a better look at the girl's face. Constance planted her elbows on her knees as she held her face in her hands. In many ways seeing her daughter was almost like looking into the past. She had Kari's hair and eyes but a different nose.

Kari glanced around the room, looking for family

photos, anything that might help explain their relationship. Photographs of flowers decorated the walls.

"Hi, Constance." Kari knelt on the floor next to the girl. Her hand shook as she reached to touch the child's hair. "Do you know who I am?"

Constance glanced at her and then back to the cartoon. "The outside lady."

Kari looked to Vivien for help as she tried to find a way to broach a conversation. She wondered if she grabbed the girl and held her close that she could force her magic to transport them somewhere safe. Unfortunately, her magical power wasn't exactly predictable or controllable.

"So what's this about a transplant?" Vivien asked. "You sick?"

Kari frowned at the bluntness, but the approach worked. She should have known to trust Vivien's ability to talk to people the way they needed to be spoken to.

Constance shrugged. "They said I'm probably ready for my new soul if my blood comes back healthy enough."

Constance grabbed the health shake as if the idea reminded her to finish it. She took a long drink.

"A new soul?" Kari leaned forward to make her daughter meet her eyes. "What does that mean?"

"I'm getting my adult soul." Constance scoffed a little as if the question were stupid. "I'm getting rid of my kid soul."

"Don't let her take the soul." Lori's plea whispered through her thoughts.

Kari felt a wave of cold rush through her. She looked at the room with its toys and cartoons and the healthy shake Constance was given to drink. Connie would have never allowed this...unless she didn't expect Constance to need an education.

"Honey, that's not..." Kari took a deep breath. The fear inside her built. What if Constance rejected her as a mother? What if they couldn't save her?

"You shouldn't call me that," Constance said. "You'll get fired."

"Oh, baby, no," Kari whispered. "This is not how things are supposed to be."

Constance picked up the remote and turned the television off as the credits began to roll. She stood and glanced at Heather and Vivien before she studied Kari's face. She put one of her small hands on Kari's shoulder. "Why are you crying? Are you hurt?"

"I'm scared," Kari said, covering the hand with hers.

"Oh." Constance looked at Vivien and Heather

again. "Do you want to see what makes me feel better?"

Kari nodded.

Constance went to a small nightstand and opened a drawer. She took out a worn picture and brought it to Kari. It was of Kari in a formal gown for her high school prom. "This is my mother. She's dead. You look like her, though. Are you related to her?"

"Where did you get this?" Kari asked.

"Mrs. Connie gave it to me," Constance said.

Kari held the picture next to her face. "This is me from a long, long time ago. I'm your mother. You're my daughter."

Constance started to shake her head in denial. A hurried knock sounded on the door before Kari could convince the girl of the truth.

Heather's eyes rounded. "We're not alone. I sense Connie is close."

Kari kept hold of Constance's hand as she stood. The chill inside her deepened like a block of ice sitting inside her chest.

The door opened. She expected to see Sue and Lorna. Instead, Mrs. Willow entered with two exceedingly tall men who looked better suited to being bouncers. The material of their blue scrubs strained against their muscles as they crossed their arms over their chests.

"Hi, Mrs. Willow. Hi, Carl. Hi, Dave." Constance didn't sound excited to see them.

The men nodded as she said their names.

Dave's brow furrowed, and the severeness of his expression accentuated the trimmed lines of his buzz cut. His appearance terrified her less than Carl's. The smaller of the two giants, Carl smiled and flexed his fingers as if just waiting for the order to pounce.

"It's time to go," Mrs. Willow ordered.

Heather and Vivien moved to shield Kari and Constance from view. Kari looked out the open bedroom door but couldn't see Sue and Lorna. She prayed they were all right.

"She's not ready," Heather said.

"Go ahead. We'll bring her to you," Vivien added.

"It is time for *you all* to go," Mrs. Willow clarified. "Before we have you arrested for trespassing and attempted kidnapping."

"Us arrested?" Vivien snorted in disgust, dropping her pleasant façade. "You're one to talk, lady. Go ahead, call the police. Let them see this little cult you have going here."

"Medical staff," Mrs. Willow corrected.

"Call them," Vivien insisted.

"Dave." Mrs. Willow lifted her hand and gestured toward Heather and Vivien. "Remove them."

Dave dropped his arms and stepped forward. Heather and Vivien stood their ground.

"I told you they'd fire you." Constance tried to pull her hand away.

Kari tightened her hold on her daughter's hand and willed her magic to transport them out of there. Under her breath, she pleaded, "Come on, magic. Transport us."

Nothing happened.

Dave lunged toward Vivien. She drew her arms inward, rotated, and side kicked him in the stomach. Dave grunted but absorbed the blow. He grabbed her ankle before she could fully retract the kick and lifted it into the air. Vivien cried out in pain as she lost her balance. Her hands landed on the floor with hard thuds to stop her fall.

"Don't you touch her!" Heather tried to come to Vivien's defense, but Carl sprang forward. She shoved the flat of her palm toward his nose, barely missing as it glanced against his cheek. With a few deft moves, the man strong-armed her into easy submission.

Constance yelped and buried her head against Kari's hip. Kari held her tighter.

"Kari, get her out of here!" Vivien yelled. "Run!"

Kari tried, but Mrs. Willow blocked the door.

"Don't make this difficult," Mrs. Willow warned.

"She's just a child!" Heather squirmed against her captor. "You know this isn't right."

"And you are trespassers." Mrs. Willow watched dispassionately as Vivien and Heather were dragged, kicking and protesting from the room. Loud thuds sounded in the hallway as they continued to fight. When they were alone, the caretaker said, "Rhode Island is very forgiving about people protecting themselves in their own homes, and our employer has very deep pockets. Be grateful you're escaping today with your lives."

"Go ahead, call the police. Do it." Kari wondered if she could charge past Mrs. Willow without endangering Constance. "I'd love for you to explain to them why you're holding my daughter hostage."

"This kid is an orphan, and she lives better than most adults," Mrs. Willow countered.

"How can you live with yourself? You know what Connie has planned, don't you?" Kari demanded. "You know what a soul transplant means."

"If my employer wants to say a few chants and burn some incense as a rite of passage, that's on her. She pays me not to ask questions. At the end of the day, my ward is right where she needs to be." Mrs. Willow held her hand toward Constance. "Come on. It's time to be a big girl. You know there's nothing to be afraid of, don't you, Constance?"

"Go to hell," Kari countered.

Mrs. Willow frowned.

"Are you really my mother?" Constance asked.

"Yes." Kari nodded. "And I've come to take you home with me."

"Dave!" Mrs. Willow yelled.

Dave reappeared alone. This time he held a handgun and pointed it at her chest. "Release the child."

"What did you do to my friends?" Kari backed away. There was no getting past the armed giant.

"Constance, you know the rules. Obey, or we'll have to call Connie," Mrs. Willow pointed toward the open door. "Come on. It's time."

Kari tried to hold on to her daughter.

"Can I see her afterward?" Constance asked.

"Sure you can," Mrs. Willow lied. "If you do what you're told."

Constance managed to free herself and go toward them. "Don't be scared. I'll come back."

Kari squared her shoulder and ran past her daughter. She tried to ram Dave in the chest. "Don't you touch—!"

He swung his hand and knocked her on the side of her head with the butt of the gun. Pain shot through her skull. Kari stumbled, dazed, and fought to stay on her feet.

"Now, Constance," Mrs. Willow ordered.

A heavy vise clamped her arm, and Dave jerked her toward the door. Self-preservation kicked in, and white light flooded her, removing her from danger.

CHAPTER EIGHTEEN

KARI HELD HER HEAD. Her magic had transported her out of harm's way into darkness. Angrily, she muttered, "Oh, sure, now you fucking decide to work."

"Kari?" Sue whispered. "Is that you?"

Kari turned in the darkness. "Sue?"

"Yes," Sue answered. "I'm here."

"All of us are," Lorna added.

Kari reached out her hands and felt around in the darkness, trying to find a light switch. Her fingers met a doorknob. She turned it slowly, but it was locked. "Where are you?"

A muffled sound answered her.

"We're on the floor," Heather said. "Can you untie us?"

Kari knelt and felt her way toward their voices.

Her head throbbed. She came in contact with a shoe. She ran her fingers upward to find a pair of ankles tied with a thick plastic zip tie. "It's too tight. I can't."

"I have a pocketknife in my boot," Heather said, thumping her feet a few times. "We've been trying to get to it."

Kari moved toward Heather. The woman was turned on her side. Kari dug her fingers into the boot.

"Other one, inside leg," Heather directed.

"I'm sorry we weren't able to warn you better," Sue said. "They caught us in the hallway. That bitch Mrs. Willow checked on our employment and they knew we were intruders."

Kari found the knife and pulled it out. She fumbled to feel how to open the blade. "Is anyone hurt?"

"Bruised," Heather answered. "We'll live."

Kari pulled the knife open and gently guided it to Heather's bound feet. She cut the zip tie.

"Vivien?" Kari asked since the woman hadn't spoken. A muffled voice answered.

"They gagged her," Lorna said. "She bit one of them."

"Where's Constance?" Sue asked. "Is she safe?"

Guilt and fear flooded her at the question. Kari cut

Heather's wrists free. "Mrs. Willow took her. I couldn't stop them."

"We'll get her back," Lorna said.

"I filled them in on what is happening." Heather ran her hand down Kari's arm. "Give me the knife. I'll do it."

Kari turned the blade downward to hand Heather the handle without cutting her. Heather began freeing the others.

"We tried yelling, but I don't think anyone out there cares," Sue said.

"That's because they're a cult," Heather grumbled.

"I should have transported us out of here the second we found Constance." Kari gingerly fingered the wound on her head, feeling the tackiness of drying blood. The dizziness was beginning to make her nauseous. "I tried after you were taken, but nothing happened. The magic only brought me here when one of those thugs was hurting me."

"Everything happens for a reason," Lorna said. "Maybe you need to be here."

Vivien gasped and coughed. "Oh, those bastards."

Kari went back to the door and retried the knob. A part of her wanted to fall to her knees and weep, to give in to the pounding in her head, but another feeling overtook every weakness inside her. Constance. She needed to save her daughter.

Kari had never daydreamed about what it would feel like to be a mother. Then learning she had a daughter, it had been more of a surreal concept than a reality. But seeing her, touching her, hearing her little voice... Kari choked back tears.

"We'll find her." Vivien located Kari in the dark and gave her a small hug.

"Why can't I control this stupid power?" Kari leaned her head against Vivien's shoulder.

"It's new. You'll figure it out," Vivien promised. "But for now, how about you depend on your friends? We're not going to let Connie win. Now, give me your hand."

Kari held her hand. She couldn't see, but she could feel Vivien connecting to Sue, then Sue to Heather, and then Heather to Lorna. Each woman had her own special vibration, like a signature unique to them. She'd felt it when they did the séance, but also whenever they touched. It formed a closer bond.

"We want to go to Constance," Vivien said. The vibrations between them built. "Kari, take us to Const—"

The bright light of her magic flashed, and they moved as a group from the dark closet into the candlelight. It took Kari a moment to get her bearings. The house staff cult members stood in their blue scrubs, turned away from where they materialized. Sickly yellow candles formed an infinity symbol—one loop around Constance and the other empty. The flames gave off a foul odor.

Kari started forward, but Vivien kept ahold of her hand and pulled her back.

"Connie, join us. Accept your vessel," Mrs. Willow summoned, tilting her head back to look at the ceiling. Connie appeared in the second loop. The candlelight slithered around the infinity symbol like a snake.

Kari felt her resentment build. Connie looked as she had when she performed her first hex, the night Julia had warned her to stop dabbling in black magic. That was the night this whole thing started.

She felt Lorna break their human chain only to appear next to her. Lorna put her hand against Kari's wounded head and reached her hand toward Mrs. Willow. Kari instantly understood as they all took a step closer. The movement startled several of the staff, and they turned in surprise.

Lorna shoved her hand against the back of Mrs. Willow's head. Kari felt instant relief as the headache flowed out of her body. Her bruised, injured knuckles from Lori's possession healed as they passed over. But it wasn't just the headache and aching knuckles that moved through Lorna to Mrs. Willow. It was Vivien's tender ribs and the cut on her hand, Heather's aching knee and back, and Sue's period cramps. She detected the pain from Vivien's jaw from the tight gag, an old cut on Heather's arm, Sue's toothache, even the itchy stitches in her own leg and the leftover soreness in her muscles. No matter how small, Lorna gave every pain or discomfort to the awful woman.

Mrs. Willow cried out and grabbed her head. Lorna dropped her hand and resumed her place in their chain.

"Back off, bitches, or you're next!" Lorna yelled.

The staff parted in confusion as they looked to the screeching Mrs. Willow for direction. When they didn't receive it, they began to scatter.

Connie ignored the chaos as she stared intently at Constance. The child began to cry. Constance stood and tried to leave the infinity loop, but an invisible force stopped her.

Kari let go of Vivien and ran at the candles. She leaped over them, entering the loop.

"Stop!" Connie ordered, her stern voice causing the floor to shake. The candlelight jiggled.

Kari grabbed hold of Constance and lifted her into her arms. "Fuck you, Connie!"

Kari glanced at her friends. The magic surged, and she willed them all to travel back to Freewild Cove. They materialized inside the Warrick Theater on the black-painted stage.

"Holy crap," Sue exclaimed. "That was terrifying."

"What are we doing here?" Lorna asked.

"I didn't want to bring her to Connie's house," Kari answered. "This was the only place I could think of that felt safe."

"No, it's good." Vivien looked around and yelled, "Grandma Julia, you here? We could use your help!"

Constance continued to sniffle as Kari set her on her feet.

"Hey, hey, it's okay," Kari soothed, leaning over to be at the girl's eye level. "You're safe. I'm not going to let anything happen to you."

"I don't want an adult soul," Constance managed between gasping breaths. "It hurt."

"You're not going to get one," Kari promised. "And you never, ever, ever will be in a place like that again."

"I don't mean to interrupt, but Julia is saying to get ready for company." Heather ran to look behind the curtain. "Lorna, do we have any extra summoning candles back here? Anything?"

"No. I think all the extras are at the house in the

trunk of the car." Lorna went to join Heather in the search. "If we did, they'd be right here."

"We'll have to summon Julia without the candles," Heather said. "She wants to help."

"Can we do that?" Kari asked.

"It won't be as easy, but Julia won't need the props," Vivien stated. "Thanks to Lorna taking our ailments; we all should have extra energy to burn."

It was true. Lorna's magic had left Kari feeling physically better than she had in years.

"Constance, honey," Heather came to the girl. "I know you're frightened right now, but we're going to make things better. I need you to stay close to your mom, all right?"

Constance nodded but still looked scared.

"Good girl. We're not going to let anyone harm you. I promise," Vivien added.

The women joined hands while Constance hugged close to Kari's leg.

Kari smiled reassuringly at the girl as the others chanted, "Spirits tethered to this plane, we humbly seek your guidance. Spirits, search amongst your numbers for the spirit we seek. We call forth Julia Warrick from the great beyond."

"You gals sure stirred a hornet's nest this time."

Julia Warrick's voice appeared before she did. They released each other's hands.

Constance whimpered as Julia materialized on the stage. The sound drew Julia's attention.

"Your death is gone," Julia stated, looking Kari over. The ghost wore high-waisted trousers from the nineteen-twenties and a matching vest over a dressier blouse. Her short bob looked straight out of the silent film era. "Good."

"I promise to fill you in completely later," Heather said, "but right now, we need your help. Your old friend is trying to pull a forced reincarnation."

"What's to explain?" Julia asked with a bored wave. A cigarette in a long holder appeared between her lips. She took a long drag before pulling it away to let phantom smoke roll out of her mouth. It didn't give off a smell as it disappeared inches above her head. "Kari has the ring I left for Lori's protection. The fact that she's here means Connie's up to her old tricks. Where is the old bat?"

"Dead," Vivien answered.

"Can't say that's a bad thing," Julia dismissed.

"You said we were about to have company," Heather prompted.

"Did I?" Julia shrugged, as if not remembering.

"Connie hexed my parents," Kari said. "The night you left this ring."

Julia's outfit blurred as she came closer, turning into the green dress with large white flowers she wore the night Connie had cast her spell over Lori.

"I'm so sorry, love," Julia said. Her face had aged some, and she looked less feisty. "The magic she summoned killed your mother. I warned her a severing spell would not do what she wanted. Connie thought she could keep them apart, but she underestimated the depth of your parents' love. Unfortunately, death was the only thing that could sever—the connection anyway, but not the feelings. If she killed them both, they'd be together in the afterlife, but killing one of them kept them apart."

"You couldn't tell us this before?" Heather demanded, saying what Kari was thinking.

"Before, I was a little preoccupied with the cosmic ooze clinging to her," Julia defended. "It's not often my granddaughter tries to introduce me to a vengeful spirit with recent death on her hands. Those things will suck everything dry—even us livelier spirits. How was I to know she was a vessel and not the actual vengeful ghost?"

"I don't want to be a vessel," Constance cried.

"You won't be." Kari pulled her daughter closer.

"Her?" Julia frowned. "Connie is trying to get into a child?"

Heather nodded.

"I should have known." Julia frowned. "I thought she'd learned her lesson after the death of her—"

"Oh, Julia, don't tell me this is where you have been spending your eternity." Connie appeared walking down the aisle between the rows of chairs. "I can't tell if that's just sad or pathetic."

Constance gave a half-moan, half-scream of panic. Vivien, Heather, Sue, and Lorna instantly surrounded the girl to create a shield blocking her from Connie's view.

Connie glanced in Kari's direction. "I'll deal with you in a minute."

"Stay here," Kari whispered to Constance.

Lorna instantly hugged the girl close to her, hiding her behind the wall the others made with their body.

Kari strode toward the center stage to face Connie's approach. "I guess we know why you put the bulk of the fortune in a trust."

Connie laughed. "I'm nothing if not pragmatic."

"That's not the word I would use for you." Kari knew she should be frightened. There was no invisible field to keep Connie contained.

"You know the great thing about being dead? I

don't have to listen to you whine." Connie glided up the stairs.

Julia appeared next to Kari. "You're not getting that child."

"She's already mine. The spell is done." Connie eyed Kari. "And I can tell you that the first chance I get, I'm running away from home. When this is over, we're over. You should have never been born. I'm through. I wash my hands of you."

Kari's lip curled in disgust. "No, Connie. I'm done with you. I'm taking my daughter, and we're going to live in the RV traveling the world. I'll make sure she forgets all about you."

A chill worked its way over Kari as Connie loomed closer. "Try to stop me."

"Thought you'd never ask," Julia stated.

Connie laughed in dismissal. "Please, if this two-bit hack is the best you got—"

"Girls, the spell you used with Lorna's pest," Julia interrupted. "Now."

"Being tethered to this plane," Heather and Vivien said in unison.

Connie's expression changed into one of panic. "What?"

"Full of rage and filled with pain," Lorna and Sue joined in on the chant.

Kari merely smiled, not knowing the words. She went to stand with Constance.

Julia's form began to grow brighter.

"We call you to come near," they continued. "We call you to face what you fear. We call you to your eternal hell."

Julia surged forward, slamming her body into Connie to shove her off the stage. Connie's spirit flailed through the air.

"Pay the price with this final knell," Julia chanted with the others.

Connie let loose a loud screech. Flames erupted over her thrashing body. The awful noise grew as Connie flew over the seats, trying to outrun her fate. She shot through the air, coming straight at Kari and Constance. Kari curled her body around her daughter in protection from the flames. Connie crashed into her back and instantly dissipated into smoke and ash. Heat rushed over her but didn't burn.

When she stood, Kari saw a gray dust coating the parts of her friends that had been exposed to Connie's final attack. She felt it falling from her hair as she moved.

"Please tell me we're not covered in Connie." Kari grimaced.

"I like to think of it more like demon dust." Vivien patted Kari on the shoulder, stirring particles.

Kari coughed and backed away from where it swirled in the air.

"Exorcisms are not just for demons," Julia lectured. "Did you girls neglect to read all the notes I left for you?"

"What notes?" Lorna asked.

Julia waved her hand as if it didn't matter.

"No, seriously, what notes?" Lorna insisted.

"Well, I'm exhausted," Julia stated, instantly disappearing.

"Julia?" Lorna called.

"Don't bother. She's gone, and she probably just realized she actually forgot to leave us better instructions," Heather said.

"Hey, you all right?" Kari dropped to the floor to kneel by her daughter.

Constance looked around the theater. Out of all of them, she was the only one free of dust. Slowly, she nodded. "Is that lady gone for good?"

"Yes, Connie is gone for good," Kari answered. "She'll never bother you again. I promise I'll always keep you safe."

"No, the other lady," Constance said.

"That's my grandma Julia," Heather answered.

"She's not like Connie. You have nothing to worry about with her."

"I think it's safe to say we won." Vivien dusted off her arm. "I don't know about the rest of you, but I need a bath and a stiff drink. Kari, any chance you can give us a lift back to your place so that we can pick up our cars?"

"Not me." Sue hopped off the stage. "My shower is upstairs, and I should check on the bookstore. Call me if you need me. Or if you're about to transport me."

"Our house. Tonight," Lorna told Sue. "We'll decompress."

"Don't you mean debrief?" Vivien chuckled.

Heather leaned over and tried to shake the Connie demon dust out of her hair. "Call it whatever you want as long as there is wine."

"What's an RV?" Constance looked unsure. "You said I was going to live in an RV."

"It's a house with wheels," Kari answered.

At that, the girl giggled. The sound filled Kari with relief.

"Houses don't have wheels," Constance explained.

"Mine does. And it travels all around the country, wherever we want to go," Kari answered.

"To the moon?" Constance asked.

"Well, maybe not there," Kari amended.

"I'm not allowed to travel unless it's to a new house, but we only move on my birthday," Constance said.

"Not anymore." Kari patted the girl's hair, smoothing it toward her bun. She looked at the miniature scrubs. "You can also wear whatever you want and stay up late, and we'll eat junk food—not all the time but sometimes. Things are going to be different."

Kari hesitated before holding out her arms for a hug. Constance leaned into her by small degrees. The embrace didn't come naturally for Constance, and Kari silently promised to change that very soon. She might not have all the answers to motherhood, but she knew kids deserved love, and she had that to give. She also knew she would never be the type of parent Connie had been.

Vivien touched her shoulder. Kari nodded. Without much thought, she felt her magic transporting them to Connie's house. They appeared in the front entryway. Knowing Connie couldn't hurt them anymore calmed her fears, and the traveling magic didn't seem quite so difficult as before.

"Kari? Are you back?" Angel sounded panicked.

Kari released Constance from the hug and stood.

"Are you all right?" Angel came from the kitchen. "What happened? I looked for you."

"Yes, we're fine. I'm sorry I didn't call, but..."

"I'm just glad you're not hurt." Angel moved past Heather in the hallway.

Vivien leaned against the doorway to the living room, and Lorna sat down on the stairs.

Angel pulled Kari against him and held her close. His hands slipped into her dirty hair, and he pulled away to look at it.

"We're okay. Connie is gone for good this time." Kari stepped aside and put her hand on Constance's shoulder to draw her into view. He looked down in surprise to see a child. "Angel, I'd like you to meet my daughter, Constance."

"Hello, there." Angel smiled. "I'm delighted to meet you."

Constance tucked her chin while still looking up at him.

"I'm going to go poke around upstairs just to be sure nothing lingers," Heather said. Lorna leaned to the side to let her pass as Heather took the steps two at a time. Vivien moved to sit next to Lorna.

"Constance, this is my boyfriend, Angel." Kari reached for his hand. The emotions that ran through her were impossible to verbalize. Warm love flowed between them, unspoken and pure. Like with her friends, she didn't feel the need to explain how she was feeling. That one touch and he knew her heart, and she understood his.

Angel smiled at her, that same handsome smile that had first caused her heart to flutter, and she realized that she wanted to spend the rest of her life looking at his face.

Family.

Legacy. Duty. Disappointment. Blame. But not love.

She'd thought those words at Connie's funeral, in what felt like a long time ago. No longer did they ring true.

Family.

Connection. Choices. Appreciation. Love. Mostly love.

Kari had everything she'd ever wanted. Vivien, Heather, Sue, and Lorna were her sisters. Angel was her lover, her heart. And Constance, her beautiful daughter, was a piece of her soul.

Family.

Now she only needed to find her father.

"How did you find her?" Angel asked. "Where?"

"Rhode Island." Kari smiled. "I promise to tell you all about it later."

He nodded.

"All good." Heather came back downstairs. "Nothing left here but drywall and some wood rot."

"Hey, Kari, we're going to take off," Vivien said. "We have some neglected boyfriends who'll want a little attention."

"Call us if you need us," Lorna added. "I'd invite you over tonight, but I have a feeling you're going to be busy."

The women said goodbye to Constance and left. Kari heard the sound of car doors in the driveway.

"I don't know about you ladies, but I'm starving," Angel said. "What do you think, Constance? Should we order a pizza?"

"What's a pizza?" Constance asked.

Angel looked surprised. "You've never had a pizza?"

Constance shook her head in denial.

"Well, I think that's something we need to rectify immediately." He looked at Kari. "If it's okay with your mom."

Kari nodded. Dust drifted from her hair.

"Great, you go get cleaned up." He gestured to indicate her dirty hair before turning to Constance. "And we'll order dinner off my cellphone. You can pick out anything you want, but I'm going to have to recommend the pepperoni, extra cheese."

Kari watched as Constance followed Angel toward the kitchen. It occurred to her that the child might be a little too trusting when it came to strangers, but then Constance had been raised by them.

"This house doesn't have wheels," Constance stated.

"No, it doesn't," Angel laughed. "But the one out back does."

Kari made her way upstairs. Instead of going to the bathroom, she found herself in the storage room. She flipped on the light and stared at the empty space. The air felt normal, all oppression and heaviness gone. In fact, the entire house felt different. It was just an old house in need of repairs.

"Mom, I don't know if you can hear me since you've moved on. I wanted to thank you. I found my daughter, and she is so beautiful. I wish you could have met her." Kari walked to stand next to the patched floor. "She has your nose."

Kari listened, but the room remained silent.

"I forgive you for using me to hurt Connie. I know it wasn't you, not really. I want you to know she can't hurt anyone ever again. We did it. We stopped her."

Kari held her hand parallel to the floor, feeling for changes in the temperature that might indicate something was close. It remained even.

"All that's left is to find my father. Angel's cousin is a private investigator. He's looking into it. I won't stop until I find him. I'm going to tell him everything."

Kari closed her eyes. Tears slid over her cheeks. She wanted to see her mom one more time.

"I'm going to take Constance with me on the road and homeschool her. I don't think she's seen much of the world, and I have a feeling her education has been lacking if you can believe that with Connie. I'm going to ask Angel to come with me. I think he will."

Kari opened her eyes and backed toward the door. She flipped off the lights and peered into the dark.

"Anyway, Mom, I wanted you to know that I love you." She took a deep breath. "And your family is going to be okay."

CHAPTER NINETEEN

KARI WATCHED Constance play with Jingles on her bunk bed. With Angel and Constance on the road with her, it had been time for Kari to upgrade to a bigger RV. Sliders extended to make a living room and kitchen, and wider bedroom. The extra space was nice, but they spent little time inside. The world was a big and beautiful place, and Kari wanted to show Constance all of it.

Years of educational neglect showed in some of the girl's lessons, but Kari tried to keep learning fun and the pressure off. One good thing Kari could say about Constance's upbringing was that the girl enjoyed health food and exercise. She also had a curiosity that couldn't be sated.

Without paychecks, all of Constance's caretakers had disbanded. No one contested Kari's rights, and she was able to fast-track legal custody of her daughter. The suit against the Alcott-Grove fertility wing was going to take longer, but she wanted to make sure they never, ever, violated a woman's medical rights again. Money didn't buy happiness, but there were some things that money could provide—like expedited legal help.

There was no record of Constance's father, not that the girl seemed to notice. She'd taken to referring to Angel as her dad.

After a heated conversation between Vivien and her lawyer ex-husband, Kari had been named trustee to the Alcott-Grove millions. It seemed fitting to spend Connie's fortune undoing the evil she had performed in life, which went beyond what she'd done to her family. When they went by the Mississippi furniture store, the working conditions hadn't been great. Kari had instantly rectified that. With Vivien's psychic help, they'd hired all new management. Kari was in the process of going through all of the other assets.

Kari grabbed the coffee pot and poured two mugs before taking them outside. The cool morning breeze coming off the nearby lake welcomed her. Other people camped in nearby RVs along the shore in designated parking spots. It wasn't her favorite location, crammed into a makeshift camping city, but today she didn't care.

Angel sat at a picnic table talking on the phone. "Yes, Mamá, we're just right outside of Nashville."

"Tell her I say hello," Kari said softly.

"Kari says hi." Angel flashed Kari a smile as she set down a mug by him. He lowered the phone and answered, "She says hello."

Kari sat next to him and held the coffee in her hands. She heard Constance's giggle coming from inside, followed by the tinkling of Jingle's collar. Nervous energy bubbled inside her, and she ended up tapping her nails against the ceramic mug.

"I told you, I plan on asking her to marry me tonight," Angel said into the phone.

Kari gave a small laugh and arched a brow at him.

He shrugged and mouthed. "Want to?"

Kari returned his shrug but couldn't contain her smile. "Tell her I plan on saying yes when you ask me later."

A sedan rolled down the gravel road toward them, kicking up a small layer of dust as it slowly passed by the other RVs. Her ring finger began to vibrate in warning. Kari put her mug down and stood.

"Mamá, I have to go. I'll call you later." Angel hung up the phone. "Do you think that's him?"

Kari held up her vibrating hand and nodded. She moved around the table as the car neared. Her heartbeat quickened, and she found it difficult to breathe.

The moment he opened the car door and stepped out, Kari recognized him. Age had crawled over his face, and gray invaded his once mohawked hair, but it was him—her father.

It took him a long moment to shut the car door as he stared at her.

Kari took a nervous step forward. She lifted her hand. "Hi, Derek, um, Dad. I'm Kari Grove. Your daughter."

He stared at her and didn't move.

"I'm so glad you came," she insisted.

Still, he held silent.

"They told me you don't have a phone," she explained, "or I would have called instead of sending a private investigator to track you down."

"Don't have much use for a phone." Derek reached for the door handle as if to leave. "I'm sorry. This was selfish. I shouldn't have come. It's not safe."

"Connie's gone," Kari stated, hurrying forward to stop him from leaving. "Dead."

He dropped his hand and looked at her.

"It doesn't matter. The things she can do surpasses death. Just going near Lori..." Emotion overwhelmed Derek's expression, and he choked on his words. "Connie warned me to stay away from your mother, but I didn't believe her. She didn't think I was good enough for her daughter. She's dead because of me."

"I know about the hex. I know Connie probably warned you to stay away from me, or you'd kill me too, but none of that matters now. Connie is gone, and all her evil has gone with her." Kari continued forward and reached out her hand. "It's okay, Dad."

He watched her hand come near and didn't reach for her. Kari touched his arm. He gasped as if expecting her to fall dead at his feet. When she didn't, he gave a pained moan and grabbed her against his chest.

"I can't believe..." His words were barely coherent, and he began to cry. "I dreamed of this since the day you were born."

"I have so much I want to share with you," Kari whispered.

"Is that my grandpa?" Constance yelled from the RV.

"Grandpa?" Derek pulled away and looked past Kari. His hands shook.

"I want to introduce you to your family." Kari

walked with her father toward the picnic table. He held her hand against his arm, as if not wanting to let her go.

Angel stood, smiling in greeting. "It's an honor to meet you, sir. I'm Angel."

Derek shook his hand. "Derek."

"Grandpa, come on," Constance shot forward in excitement to tug at his arm. "I want you to meet Jingles."

Derek chuckled as she pulled him into the RV. "Jingles, you say? That's a strange name for a brother."

"He's my cat!" Constance laughed.

Tears fell from Kari's eyes.

Angel pulled her into his arms in a sturdy hug. "You okay?"

Kari nodded. "I have more than I've ever dreamed possible."

Angel kissed her briefly before walking with her toward the RV to join the others inside. "You deserve every happiness, Kari."

She smiled. The last of Connie's curse died as Kari heard her father talking to her daughter. "This is all I've ever wanted. A true family."

The End

The Magical Fun Continues!
Order of Magic Book 6
The Seventh Key

GET THE BOOKS!

THE MAGICAL FUN CONTINUES!

Lorna's Story: Second Chance Magic

Vivien's Story: Third Time's a Charm

Heather's Story: The Fourth Power

Sue's Story: The Fifth Sense

Kari's Story: The Sixth Spell

Next Books:
The Seventh Key
The Eighth Potion

ABOUT MICHELLE M. PILLOW

New York Times & *USA TODAY*
Bestselling Author

Michelle loves to travel and try new things, whether it's a paranormal investigation of an old Vaudeville Theatre or climbing Mayan temples in Belize. She believes life is an adventure fueled by copious amounts of coffee.

Newly relocated to the American South, Michelle is involved in various film and documentary projects with her talented director husband. She is mom to a fantastic artist. And she's managed by a dog and cat who make sure she's meeting her deadlines.

For the most part she can be found wearing pajama pants and working in her office. There may or may not be dancing. It's all part of the creative process.

Come say hello! Michelle loves talking with readers on social media!

www.MichellePillow.com

PLEASE TAKE A MOMENT TO SHARE YOUR THOUGHTS BY REVIEWING THIS BOOK.

Thank you to all the wonderful readers who take the time to share your thoughts about the books you love. I can't begin to tell you how important you are when it comes to helping other readers discover the books!

facebook.com/AuthorMichellePillow

twitter.com/michellepillow

instagram.com/michellempillow

bookbub.com/authors/michelle-m-pillow

goodreads.com/Michelle_Pillow

amazon.com/author/michellepillow

youtube.com/michellepillow

pinterest.com/michellepillow

NEWSLETTER

To stay informed about when a new book in the series installments is released, sign up for updates:

Sign up for Michelle's Newsletter

michellepillow.com/author-updates

PLEASE LEAVE A REVIEW

THANK YOU FOR READING!

Please take a moment to share your thoughts by reviewing this book.

Be sure to check out Michelle's other titles at https://michellepillow.com

Made in the USA
Coppell, TX
10 December 2021